CONARD COUNTY: MURDEROUS INTENT

New York Times **Bestselling Author**

RACHEL LEE

D1056191

⬡ **HARLEQUIN**

INTRIGUE

To the far-too-many veterans who struggle daily
with reentering civilian life.

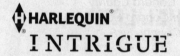

ISBN-13: 978-1-335-59156-2

Conard County: Murderous Intent

Copyright © 2024 by Susan Civil-Brown

For questions and comments about the quality of this book, please contact us at CustomerService@Harlequin.com.

TM and ® are trademarks of Harlequin Enterprises ULC.

Harlequin Enterprises ULC
22 Adelaide St. West, 41st Floor
Toronto, Ontario M5H 4E3, Canada
www.Harlequin.com

Printed in Lithuania

Recycling programs
for this product may
not exist in your area.

MIX
Paper | Supporting
responsible forestry
FSC® C021394

Rachel Lee was hooked on writing by the age of twelve and practiced her craft as she moved from place to place all over the United States. This *New York Times* bestselling author now resides in Florida and has the joy of writing full-time.

Books by Rachel Lee

Harlequin Intrigue

Conard County: The Next Generation

Visit the Author Profile page at Harlequin.com.

CAST OF CHARACTERS

Krystal Metcalfe—Writer and part owner of the Mountain Writers' Retreat in Conard County, Wyoming. She has a problem with the stockade built on the other side of the creek, a stockade that has invaded the privacy of what she calls her Zen Zone.

Josh Healey—Owner of the land across the creek. It's been in his family for generations and now he's building on it to create a safe place for veterans who are dealing with issues related to returning to regular civilian life. Josh is both a veteran himself and a licensed psychologist.

Mason Cambridge—An irritable, annoying and egotistical author of bestselling horror stories. No one is terribly surprised that he's the first murder victim, given he's made a lot of enemies.

Darlene Dana—Mason's agent on an annual visit. She is the most surprised by the murder of her number one client.

Joan Metcalfe—Krystal's mother and the other owner of the retreat where artistic types come for the peace and quiet of the woods.

Sebastian Elsin—Second murder victim.

Mary Collins—She believes Mason stole her book idea and cost her a bestseller.

Prologue

Krystal Metcalfe loved to sit on the porch of her small cabin in the mornings, especially when the weather was exceptionally pleasant. With a fresh cup of coffee and its delightful aroma mixing with those of the forest around, she found internal peace and calm here.

Across a bubbling creek that ran before her porch, her morning view included the old Healey house. Abandoned about twenty years ago, it had been steadily sinking into decline. The roof sagged, wood planks had been silvered by the years and there was little left that looked safe or even useful. Krystal had always anticipated the day when the forest would reclaim it.

Then came the morning when a motor home pulled up beside the crumbling house and a large man climbed out. He spent some time investigating the old structure, inside and out. Maybe hunting for anything he could reclaim? Would that be theft at this point?

She lingered, watching with mild curiosity but little concern. At some level she had always supposed that someone would express interest in the Healey land itself. It wasn't easy anymore to find private land on the edge of US Forest, and eventually the "grandfathering" that had left the Healey family their ownership would end because of lack of occupancy. Regardless, it wasn't exactly a large piece of land, unlikely to be useful to most, and the Forest Service would let it return to nature.

Less of that house meant more of the forest devouring the eyesore. And at least the bubbling of the creek passing through the canyon swallowed most of the sounds that might be coming from that direction now that the man was there. And it sure looked like he might be helping the destruction of that eyesore.

But then came another morning when she stepped out with her coffee and saw a group of people, maybe a dozen, camped around the ramshackle house. That's when things started to become noisy despite the sound baffling provided by the creek.

A truck full of lumber managed to make its way up the remaining ruined road on that side of the creek and dumped a load that caused Krystal to gasp. Rebuilding? Building bigger?

What kind of eyesore would she have to face? Her view from this porch was her favorite. Her other windows and doors didn't include the creek. And all those people buzzing around provided an annoying level of activity that would distract her.

Then came the ultimate insult: a generator fired up and drowned any peaceful sound that remained, the wind in the trees and the creek both.

That did it. Maybe these people were squatters who could be driven away. She certainly doubted she'd be able to write at all with that roaring generator. Her cabin was far from soundproofed.

After setting her coffee mug on the railing, she headed for the stepping stones that crossed the creek. For generations they'd been a path between two friendly families until the Healeys had departed. As Krystal crossed, she sensed people pulling back into the woods. Creepy. Maybe she ought to reconsider this trip across the creek. But her backbone stiffened. It usually did.

She walked around the house, now smelling of freshly cut wood, sure she'd have to find *someone*.

Then she found the man around the back corner. Since she was determined not to begin this encounter by yelling at the guy, she waited impatiently until he turned and saw her. He leaned over, turning the generator to a lower level, then simply looked at her.

He wore old jeans and a long-sleeved gray work shirt. A pair of safety goggles rode the top of his head. A dust mask hung around his neck. Workmanlike, which only made her uneasier.

Then she noticed more. God, he was gorgeous. Tall, large, broad-shouldered. A rugged, angular face with turquoise eyes that seemed to pierce the green shade of the trees. The forest's shadow hid the creek that still danced and sparkled in revealed sunlight behind her.

This area was a green cavern. One she quite liked.

Finally he spoke, clearly reluctant to do so. "Yes?"

"I'm Krystal Metcalfe. I live in the house across the creek."

One brief nod. His face remained like granite. Then slowly he said, "Josh Healey."

An alarm sounded in her mind. Then recognition made her heart hammer because this might be truly bad news. "This is Healey property, isn't it?" Of course it was. Not a bright question from her.

A short nod.

"Are you going to renovate this place?"

"Yes."

God, this was going to be like pulling teeth, she thought irritably. "I hope you're not planning to cut down many trees."

"No."

Stymied, as it became clear this man had no intention of beginning any conversation, even one as casual as talking about the weather, she glared. "Okay, then. Just take care of the forest."

She turned sharply on her heel without another word and made her way across the stepping stones to her own property. Maybe she should start drinking her morning coffee on the front porch of her house on the other side from the creek.

She was certainly going to have to go down to Conard City to buy a pair of ear protectors or go mad trying to do her own work when that generator once again revved up. *Gah!*

JOSH HEALEY HAD watched Krystal Metcalfe coming round the corner of his new building. Trouble? She sure seemed to be looking for it.

She was cute, pretty, her blue eyes as bright as the summer sky overhead. But he didn't care about that.

What he cared about were his troops, men and women who were escaping a world that PTSD and war had ripped from them. People who needed to be left alone to find balance within themselves and with group therapy. Josh, a psychologist, had brought them here for that solitude.

Now he had that neighbor trying to poke her nose into his business. Not good. He knew how people reacted to the mere idea of vets with PTSD, their beliefs that these people were unpredictable and violent.

But he had more than a dozen soldiers to protect and he was determined to do so. If that woman became a problem, he'd find a way to shut her down.

It was *his* land after all.

Chapter One

No.

Nearly a year later, that one word still sometimes re-sounded in Krystal Metcalfe's head. One of the few words and nearly the last word Josh Healey had spoken to her.

A simple question. Several simple questions, and the only response had been single syllables. Well, except for his name.

The man had annoyed her with his refusal to be neigh-borly, but nothing had changed in nearly a year. Well, ex-cept for the crowd over there. A bunch of invaders.

At least Josh Healey hadn't scalped the forest.

Krystal loved the quiet, the peace, the view from her private cabin at the Wyoming-based Mountain Artists' Retreat in the small community of Cash Creek Canyon. She was no temporary resident, unlike guests in the other cabins, but instead a permanent one as her mother's part-ner in this venture.

She thought of this cabin and the surrounding woods as her Zen Space, a place where she could always center herself, could always find the internal quiet that unleashed wandering ideas, some of them answers to questions her writing awoke in her.

But lately—well, for nearly a year in fact—this Zen

Space of hers had been invaded. Across the creek, within view from her porch, a fallen-down house had been renovated by about a dozen people, then surrounded by a rustic stockade.

What the hell? A fence would have done if they wanted some privacy, but a stockade, looking like something from a Western movie?

Well, she told herself as she sat on her porch, maybe it wasn't as ugly as chain-link or an ordinary privacy fence might have been. It certainly fit with the age of the community that had always been called Cash Creek Canyon since a brief gold rush in the 1870s.

But still, what the hell? It sat there, blending well enough with the surrounding forest, but weird. Overkill. Unnecessary, as Krystal knew from having spent most of her life right here. Nothing to hide from, nothing to hide. Not around here.

Sighing, she put her booted feet up on her porch railing and sipped her coffee, considering her previous but brief encounters with the landowner, Josh Healey.

Talk about monosyllabic! She was quite sure that she hadn't gotten more than a word from him in all this time. At least not the few times she had crossed the creek on the old stepping stones.

The Healey house had been abandoned like so many along Cash Creek as life on the mountainside had become more difficult. For twenty years, Krystal had hoped the house's steady decay would finally collapse the structure, restoring the surrounding forest to its rightful ownership.

Except that hadn't happened and she couldn't quite help getting irritated from the day a huge motor home had moved in to be followed by trucks of lumber, a noisy generator and a dozen or so men and women who camped in tents as they restored the sagging house. A year since then and she was still troubled by the activity over there.

The biggest question was why it had happened. The next question was what had brought the last owner of the property back here with a bunch of his friends to fill up the steadily shrinking hole in the woods.

No answers. At least none from Josh Healey. None, for that matter, from the Conard County sheriff's deputies who patrolled the community of Cash Creek Canyon. They knew no more than anyone: that it was a group residence.

The privacy of that stockade was absolute. At least the damn noise had quieted at last, leaving the Mountain Artists' Retreat in the kind of peace its residents needed for their creative work.

For a while it had seemed that the retreat might die from the noise, even with the muffling woods around. That had not happened, and spring's guests had arrived pretty much as usual, some new to the community, others returning visitors.

Much as she resented the building that had invaded her Zen Space, Krystal had to acknowledge a curiosity that wouldn't go away. A curiosity about those people. About the owner, who would say nothing about why he had brought them all there.

Some kind of cult?

That question troubled her. But what troubled her more was how much she enjoyed watching Josh Healey laboring around that place. Muscled. Hardworking. And entirely too attractive when he worked with his shirt off.

Dang. On the one hand she wanted to drive the man away. On the other she wanted to have sex with him. Wanted it enough to feel a tingling throughout her body.

How foolish could she get?

ACROSS THE CREEK, Josh Healey often noticed the woman who sat on her porch in the mornings drinking coffee. He knew her name because she had crossed the creek a few times: Krystal Metcalfe, joint owner of the artists' retreat. A pretty package of a woman, but he had no time or interest in such things these days.

Nor did he have any desire to share the purpose of his compound. It had been necessary to speak briefly with a deputy who hadn't been that curious. He imagined word had gotten around some, probably with attendant rumors, but no one out there in the community of Cash Creek Canyon, or beyond it in Conard City or County, had any need to know what he hoped he was accomplishing. And from what he could tell, no one did.

Nor did anyone have a need to know the reentry problems being faced by his ex-military residents.

Least of all Krystal Metcalfe, who watched too often and had ventured over here with her questions. Questions she really had no right to ask.

So when he saw her in the mornings, he shrugged it off. She had a right to sit on her damn porch, a right to watch whatever she could see…although the stockade fencing had pretty much occluded any nosy viewing.

But sometimes he wondered, with private amusement, just how she would respond if he crossed that creek and questioned her. Asked *her* about the hole in the woods created by her lodge and all the little cabins she and her mother had scattered through the forest.

Hah! She apparently felt she took care of her environment but he could see at least a dozen problems with her viewpoint. Enough problems that his own invasion seemed paltry by comparison.

As it was, right now he had more than a dozen vets, a number that often grew for a while, who kept themselves busy with maintaining the sanctuary itself, with cooking, with gardening. And a lot of time with group therapy, helping each other through a very difficult time, one that had shredded their lives. All of them leaving behind the booze and drugs previously used as easy crutches.

Some of his people left when they felt ready. New ones arrived, sometimes more than he had room for but always welcomed.

Most of the folks inside, male and female, knew about Krystal Metcalfe, and after he explained her harmless curiosity to them, they lost their suspicion, lost their fear of accusations.

Because his people *had* been accused. Every last one of them had been accused of something. It seemed society had no room for the detritus, the *problems*, their damn war had brought home.

He sighed and shook his head and continued around the perimeter of the large stockade. Like many of his folks here, he couldn't relax completely.

It always niggled at the back of his mind that someone curious or dangerous might try to get into the stockade. Exactly the thing that he'd prevented by building it this way in the first place.

But still the worry wouldn't quite leave him. His own remnant from a war.

He glanced at Krystal Metcalfe one last time before he rounded the corner. She appeared to be absorbed in a tablet.

Good. Her curiosity had gone far enough.

Chapter Two

The rusticity of the peaked dining room at the Mountain Artists' Retreat recalled a much earlier era. Dark wood covered the walls, wood planking covered the floor and the arched ceiling. Heavy beams bore the weight of exterior walls made of stone and glass. Two huge stone fireplaces decorated a pair of the walls. Wood tables, sofas and comfortable chairs, plus self-serve food bars, completed the room.

Even after all these years, Krystal entered it with both a sense of awe and a sense of home. She'd grown up here, she'd watched and then helped with the restoration as she grew older, and this room was as much a part of her life as the woods of the forest outside.

Once this had been a hunting lodge for those with plenty of money. Then there had been a brief stint as a ski lodge. Finally Joan Metcalfe had taken the reins and turned it into a popular retreat for artists.

Mason Cambridge, the retreat's star writer—at least according to him—showed up for lunch in the lodge's dining room along with a group of other writers. Krystal smothered a sigh the instant she saw him, then glanced at her mother, Joan. Joan offered an almost imperceptible shrug.

Well, hell, Krystal thought as she kept an eye on the

steam table and salad bar, making sure the trays remained full. Mason, a leonine man with wild gray hair, had already gathered a small coterie of admirers around his favorite table. It sat beside one of the tall windows beyond which leafy branches tossed about in a strong breeze.

Krystal had always held the sneaking suspicion that Mason's physical appearance was as much a matter of public relations as personal preference. Regardless, as Joan occasionally reminded her, Mason's frequent visits to the retreat were about the best publicity they could hope for. Bestselling authors drew young, less successful types like bees to flowers.

Oddly, Mason's followers mostly seemed to be women. Smothering a smirk, Krystal replaced a tray of sliced roast beef with a fresh one. Maybe, given Mason, it shouldn't be a surprise at all that women were drawn to him.

The other big draw at the retreat was Davis Daniels, a successful digital artist with a collection of comics to his name as well as some advertising work. A movie poster of his resided proudly in the Smithsonian art collection, no small achievement.

There was nothing oversize about Davis, however. A quiet, slender man, he was always polite when approached, always willing to offer advice and help when other artists asked.

Krystal was glad to head his way with a roast beef sandwich just the way he liked it. She had grown fond of him over the last few visits, and when she saw he had not yet made his lunch, she decided to look after him. Time had taught her that he was pretty much an introvert.

As always, he offered her a gentle smile and a sincere thank-you for her kindness in making his lunch, which didn't come as part of the retreat package. For an extra fee, dinners would be served by waitpersons, but only for the extra fee. Most residents chose the buffet. Well, except for Mason. Mason was an exception to every rule, even right now as he sent one of his admiring followers to get his lunch for him.

Waste of flesh, Krystal sometimes thought of him.

Forgetting about the food service for now, Krystal sat in a chair at Davis's table and rested her chin in her hand. "How's it going, Davis?"

He made a so-so gesture with his hand. "Nothing ever goes right the first time. I'm sure you know that."

"What are you working on this time?"

That cracked his face into a smile. "I'm loving it. Comic art with an impressionistic twist. Just wish I had more training with impressionism."

"If I know anything about you, you'll have all the training you need by the time you finish it."

He laughed. "That's the point, isn't it? Endless training and learning."

Then she started to rise. "I should go so you can eat."

"I can eat around words," he said dryly. "Don't run on my account."

Krystal glanced toward the serving bars and decided none of the trays appeared to be anywhere near empty, so she settled again, leaving the work to the people who had been hired to do it.

"How's *your* work coming?" Davis asked.

"I swear there must be a load of things I'm more capable of than writing a novel."

He swallowed, dabbed his mouth and smiled. "Then why did you decide to write one?"

"I thought I had a story to tell," she admitted.

"You had one to tell or one you *wanted* to tell?"

She bit her lip, hearing the suggestion of truth in his question. "I'm not sure anymore."

He nodded, ate another bite of his sandwich. "The problem," he said, "is turning a hobby you love into a job you're probably not going to love as much."

Krystal couldn't deny that.

"Try taking a break," he suggested. "Take the pressure off yourself for a couple of weeks. I do that as often as I can."

Which probably wasn't very often, Krystal thought. Davis had contracts to fulfill. She didn't have any of her own, though she dreamed of one, so the only way to keep moving was to push herself. Not exactly a good frame of mind for taking a restful break.

Before she could reply, an unmistakable hush spread through the dining room. The clatter of silverware ceased. Even Mason Cambridge's inevitably loud, grating voice fell silent.

Instinctively, Krystal turned to look.

And there in the front doorway stood a hulking man, one she recognized, turned into a threatening shadow by the brilliance of the day behind him. Josh Healey, a man who rarely ventured beyond his own walls. Her heart raced a bit as she wondered what had brought him out of his isolation.

He offered no introduction. He simply made a demand in a deep, angry voice.

"Who the hell maimed and put a seriously injured dog outside my stockade?"

KRYSTAL WAS THE first to move, possibly because no one else moved at all. She felt nearly as stunned as they, but she at least knew who the angry man was: Josh Healey.

"Mr. Healey," she said, trying to sound firm and strong. "What in the world makes you think anyone here would do such a thing?"

"Who else would?" He stepped into the large room, interior light at last casting human features over him. "The guy who raises sled dogs wouldn't have a reason. The couple who have all the horses wouldn't either. Sorry our presence bothers your holy retreat, but none of you is going to drive us out."

With that, he turned on his heel and marched away.

Silence followed his departure, but only briefly as a cacophony of voices rose with every kind of speculation, some with fear of the mountainous man who'd just crossed lines and walked into their quiet, safe space.

Krystal didn't even try to reassure anyone. It was pointless. They needed to talk about what had just happened, and being creative sorts, they'd probably have invented an entire story surrounding this event by nightfall's gathering here.

No way she could stop them, and what would she stop them with, anyway? She had absolutely no idea what had truly happened. Without facts, fiction won the day.

Joan, who'd been in the kitchen, waved her over. Krystal paused just long enough to exchange a smile with Davis, although he appeared considerably more withdrawn now. *Great.*

The kind of disturbance Krystal and her mother tried so hard to prevent had just occurred. One man. Apparently a badly injured dog. Who the heck would want to harm a dog, anyway, unless it was attacking? Josh was right about that.

It certainly couldn't have been anyone among their guests. Weapons of any kind were forbidden on these grounds.

Which, Krystal supposed, probably didn't mean much at all to anyone who was determined to bring one with them.

Shaking her head slightly, she met her mother in the kitchen doorway. Joan was a lovely woman in her fifties with salt-and-pepper hair always perfectly styled. Every few weeks two hairstylists drove up here from Conard City to take care of the guests and they always did an exquisite job on Joan.

Joan drew Krystal back into her office, away from the two cooks, who were already preparing the dinner menu.

"What just happened?" Joan demanded. "I only caught that man walking away. Everyone out there seemed upset."

Krystal couldn't prevent a half smile. "Not for long. The stories are already growing. Paul Bunyan, anyone?"

"Krystal!" Joan said disapprovingly, but a twinkle appeared in her blue eyes so like her daughter's. "No. Seriously. Is that the guy from across the creek?"

"The same."

"Well, I'm sure he never bothered to cross that creek before. What happened?"

As the moments passed since the scene, Krystal's stomach had begun to sink and now it sank more. The shock was gone, leaving only a fear of what had happened, of where it might lead. Of a sickening disgust over the kind of person who could maim a dog. "Somebody left an injured dog outside the stockade. I gather we're the prime suspects."

But Joan slid right past that thought. "A hurt dog? Did someone try to kill it? My God, Krys, how could anyone be so cruel?"

Krystal could think of a few. Not every person who lived in the little town of Cash Creek Canyon or its environs was naturally kind or good. The artists' retreat might provide a haven from the rest of the world, but beyond it, in Cash Creek proper and the wooded lands surrounding the small town, all kinds of people lived, some of whom she did her best to avoid.

Krystal knew her mother wasn't going to be able to blow the incident off and just enjoy tonight's yarns about it. Nor, truthfully, would she.

"I'll see what I can find out, Mom."

Joan's hand gripped her forearm. "Krys, that man…"

"Hasn't killed me yet," she said. "You know I've talked to him a couple of times."

"Not really," Joan said dryly, forgetting her worries briefly. But she let go of Krystal's arm. "Be careful. Maybe you should take someone with you."

Krystal bridled. "I'm perfectly capable of taking care of myself. Besides, I don't want to make the situation any tenser. I'll just ask what happened, okay?"

Free at last, she headed for the door and grabbed her lightweight jacket from a peg.

This time she was going to get more than a yes or no from that man.

A STORM HAD begun to move in over the mountains. Usually they would get only moderate rain, being in the mountain's rain shadow, but today looked and smelled different.

Krystal sniffed the air, felt the growing chill and decided she'd be unlikely to get back to the lodge dry after she talked to Josh Healey. No, she'd get back to her own cabin and spend the afternoon racking her brains trying to get words onto that damn page on the screen. And she'd believed she could write a novel. Hah!

Maybe some music would help. Sometimes it seemed to focus her brain, turning into a tool she ought to use more often than she did.

But first the issue with Josh Healey. If he'd been making a serious accusation, she had to defuse it. She'd heard he had a bunch of veterans behind the walls of his "sanctuary," but she didn't know what that might mean. Violent types on a hair trigger? Maybe. God knew, she'd heard enough about vets coming back from the war only to commit atrocities.

They certainly must feel paranoid to have built that huge stockade fence. Paranoia reflected in Healey's accusation just a short while ago. Once again, she wondered just what she was dealing with when she crossed the creek. Was paranoia making them dangerous?

As she walked over the stepping stones and drew closer to that stockade wall, she couldn't escape the fear that those walls were enclosing people who were capable of unimaginable horrors. A voluntary prison?

Sheesh! She tried to shake the feeling from the base of her skull, from the back of her neck. They'd been here nearly a year, she reminded herself. They'd made as small a mark on the Cash Creek area as anyone could. No reason to fear.

Unless, maybe, they felt they were under attack.

The dog.

Healey's accusation rode with her. These guys weren't going to be driven away? What had he meant?

Josh Healey apparently saw her approaching. A postern door in the wall opened and he stepped out.

Once again he didn't speak a word to her, just stood there waiting in a camo rain jacket and hood, hands hanging at his sides. His splayed and powerful legs made him look as immovable as the mountains that surrounded them.

At last, realizing she was going to have to start this conversation or stand there waiting until winter returned in a few months, she drew a deep breath. It was more like a sigh, probably because she'd visited this place and this man before. A possibly hopeless task was ahead.

"What happened?" she asked without preamble.

"I told you."

God, she was getting sick of his taciturnity even though their meetings had been few. "Damn it," she said impatiently, "you stomped into our lodge, made something very much like an accusation and offered no useful information!"

His head tilted a bit. His aquamarine eyes showed a glimmer of interest. "I don't recall leaving out any salient information."

So Paul Bunyan here was educated. And so what? "You said someone maimed a dog and dumped it outside your wall. How do you know it was dumped? Why should you think anyone at the retreat had anything to do with it?"

"Why shouldn't I?"

Now impatience and irritation were starting to boil into anger inside her. "Listen, Healey..."

But he interrupted her, his voice as level as a slab of

rock. "How about *you* listen for a change? The dog was dumped. How do I know? Because it had clearly been injured elsewhere. Not enough blood right here. It was a *message*, Metcalfe."

That poked a pin in the balloon of her anger. She blew a long breath, shoved her inky hair back from her face and regarded him.

When she came right down to it, the only reasons she had to be annoyed by this man and his stockade were her *own* feelings about him and this fortress he'd built. After a year, some of it noisy to be sure, she couldn't remember a single thing anyone over here had done to bother another soul.

Letting go of her anger, she studied Healey in a different light. He'd done not one thing to earn her dislike since he'd finished building this place. Not one.

What kind of story had she been building about him during all this time? Well, it would have helped if he'd made any effort to have a civil conversation. Which was ridiculous as an accusation. Nobody was required to talk with her or anyone else. She forced herself to plunge ahead anyway.

"Why are you so sure it's a message to you, Healey? No one around here has a thing against you."

"You think not?" He stared past her, into the woods, into the leaden day that was steadily shrouding the trees with a gray fog. Then those disturbing aquamarine eyes settled on her again.

"The problem," he said flatly, "is that you people think you have a right to an open book. Sorry, you don't. What goes on inside these walls, on *my* property, is no one else's business. Speculate all you want, but it's still the private business of those who live here."

"And that makes you think someone would want to make you leave? Because of one dog? That's ridiculous."

His jaw set. "What's next, Ms. Metcalfe? Another injured animal? A dead one? All to make us look bad?"

She shook her head, wanting to deny it, but unable to escape the sense that he might be right. "How's the dog?"

"I took him back to his owner. Alive. What did you think I'd do?"

Then Josh Healey appeared to tense as he continued speaking, his voice growing hard. "People distrust us because they don't know us. They don't have the right to know us."

"But if you could explain a little…"

"I don't have to explain anything." Then he stabbed a finger at her. "Has it occurred to any one of you, just *one* of you, that these walls have been built not to keep us in, but to keep the rest of you out?"

He pivoted, heading back for the door.

She took one last chance to head this conversation in a better direction. "We've gotten off on the wrong foot."

He paused, glancing over his broad shoulder. "Have we? Maybe it's been indirect, but it's clear to me that you think our mere presence is an invasion."

She nearly winced at his use of the word *invasion* because she *had* been thinking of them as invaders.

He waved an arm. "Ours." He pointed across the creek. "Yours. No reason we ever have to meet. Unless someone throws another wounded animal outside our walls."

She looked down, acknowledging that he was right, fearing she had just received an indirect threat but unsure. This guy kept her off balance somehow, and she didn't like it. "Okay. But *why* are you so sure it's a message, Mr. Healey?"

"Why else would anyone drag that injured animal to our wall? Think about it, Ms. Metcalfe."

Then he turned and walked back into his stockade, leaving her to wonder how she could be so wrong. Or maybe so right?

Maybe someone had a grudge against someone inside that stockade. Maybe the people inside had drawn danger to Cash Creek Canyon.

She turned to recross the stepping stones and tried not to think of someone stalking these woods seeking vengeance.

She looked around as she reached her cabin and shivered, as if the day had suddenly turned colder. The first splatters of icy rain hit her face.

The woods no longer seemed as friendly.

Chapter Three

As Krystal had anticipated, the evening gathering in the lodge's great room turned into a storytelling speculation. Since the food was served by the help Joan hired for those who had paid for the service or self-served by the rest, and since the cash bar was open for its usual several hours, Krystal sat back with a small brandy and watched all the byplay.

It always interested her when these largely reclusive artists actually got together to talk. Usually they separated into small groups, but not this evening. As a storm decided to hurl large raindrops against the tall glass windows, the two fires in the fireplaces made the room feel cozy. A safe place surrounded by the dark and possibly frightening woods. Probably the same atavistic response experienced by humans for hundreds of thousands of years in all its variations.

Krystal wondered with mild amusement just how many of these people were going back to their solitary cabins tonight, and how many would create pajama parties so they didn't need to be alone.

Except for Mason Cambridge, of course, who appeared to believe he had the only correct answers for what had happened that day. He would naturally hold forth for hours, weaving some story or other, and only when his admiring coterie diminished to nothing would he stagger back to his cabin.

Krystal noticed one small woman who avoided Mason's cadre and sat watching from the edges of the group in the room, her face almost frozen. With dislike, Krystal thought, but when she glanced again the woman's way, the expression had eased to one of disinterest.

Mary Collins, she remembered from previous years. A novelist who had evidently published one volume for a romance publisher. She felt as if Mary thought that was a comedown.

From Krystal's perspective, any publication of a novel was far from a comedown. However, Mary seemed bitter in a subtle way, unlike the rest of their guests, most of whom seemed hopeful or at worst frustrated by difficulties with their art.

Shrugging it aside, she returned her attention to a growing, and somewhat unpleasant, myth about the stockade and in particular Josh Healey. Of course, the way he had appeared earlier, looking almost like a threat on the hoof, she supposed it was hardly surprising.

And of course, Mason was leading the darkest version of the story.

Naturally. Didn't he write horror and suspense? Krystal thought she should be embarrassed to admit she'd never read one of his books. It seemed *everyone* read them but she'd never felt the least inclination beyond a couple of pages.

But in the midst of the growing night's storm, the front door opened again. This time no mountain man appeared, but the more familiar sight of Harris Belcher, slim and work-hardened. Wrapped in rain gear, he made a yellow splash against the orangish glow of firelight and the dimmer glow of electric lanterns and rustic chandeliers. He owned the sled dog business and pretty much knew everyone in Cash Creek Canyon including some of the regulars at the retreat.

He closed the door behind himself, throwing back the hood of his jacket. "Okay," he said. "You should all know. Somebody maimed one of my dogs today. For sure he was in his kennel, so someone took him out to injure him. His romping days are over."

Mason cleared his throat loudly, then spoke equally loudly. "What should this have to do with us? Do you think we hurt it?"

Harris put his hand on his hip. "Aren't you the self-important jackass who comes here every year? Not that I care. I think you all should know because the truth is, in all the decades I've been raising, training and sledding with my huskies and malamutes, no one has ever harmed a single one. And never, ever, taken one out of the kennel to hurt it."

"So?" Mason demanded irritably. Of course, Harris's dismissal of him had annoyed him.

"So there's someone out there being violent in a way I've never seen around here before. You need to be on guard. God knows what'll be injured next."

Krystal rose, ignoring the chill his words seemed to have thrown into the room. He had caused people to glance around at one another almost suspiciously and the mood needed some kind of redirection. "I'm really sorry, Harris. How did you find out about it?"

"That guy from the stockade. He brought Reject to me

and explained how they'd found him. They'd given him the first aid they could. Probably saved his life. Anyway, didn't take long for one of my dogs to find the killing spot and it weren't nowhere near my kennels. Or that stockade over there."

Harris dropped his hand from his hip. "No reason to hurt that dog. And no reason, I guess, for anyone to hurt you folks. Won't hurt to be on guard, though."

Joan appeared from the back. "Stay awhile, Harris. Have a drink. This has to have been quite a shock."

"Shock doesn't begin to cover it," Harris said harshly. He pushed his shaggy blond hair back from his face and looked around the room. "I'd like to think none of you might do such a thing."

"Well, what about those guys over in the stockade?" Mason demanded. "If anyone's capable of violence, it's them."

Oh, God, Krystal thought. Something inside her leaped forward like a tiger busting out of a cage. This crap had to stop *now*.

She stood as tall as she could and spoke in a loud voice she seldom used. "What are you all going to do? Start a damn witch hunt? Those vets have been over there in that stockade for a year now and there's never been a problem with any of them. Probably less trouble than some of us around here cause!"

Mason scoffed. "What would you know?"

"I've been living right across the creek from them since the day that Josh Healey first arrived. That's longer than any of *you*. Certainly longer than you, Mason. They're not some horror novel to be written."

Silence answered her. Some of the artists shifted uncomfortably, facing what they had been slowly beginning to do.

Harris Belcher, who had begun sipping beer from a handled glass mug, was the first to speak. "I'd say that bringing my dog to me was a kindness so I didn't have to keep wondering, so I could save a lot of his suffering. I'd say giving him all that first aid was true kindness, 'cuz they didn't have to. And I'd say that dumping Reject outside those stockade walls *wasn't* a kind thing to do. Somebody's got a grudge going."

Mary surprised everyone by speaking. She was one of the dourest guests they'd ever had. "Seems like those vets might have a hell of a grudge." Then she rose, grabbed her coat and left.

Another silence filled the room. Then, rain or not, people gathered up their gear and began to trail back to their cabins. Few appeared to have anything more to say, even to each other.

In the end, no one was left except a handful of staff, Joan, Harris and Krystal. The three of them settled at the bar, Krystal with her brandy, Harris with his beer and Joan with white wine.

Joan spoke first. "I'm beginning to feel as if I'm caught up in a bad movie. This whole day has been weird, and the rain outside isn't helping. All we need is some thunder to finish setting the scene."

Harris sighed. "I'm sorry, Joan. I guess I shouldn't have come over."

"You were angry, Harris. And as long as you've had your sledding business here, there's no reason to think anyone would suddenly take exception to your dogs. Of course you looked at outsiders."

"But not the folks in the stockade," Krystal pointed out. Despite her discussion earlier with Josh Healey, she couldn't quite shake her uneasiness about that place and what might go on behind those stockade walls. What they might imprison inside.

The whole place was a strange setup.

"Considering Josh Healey brought me my dog," Harris said, "I'm fairly sure he and his crew didn't have anything to do with it. For God's sake, they could have just buried Reject and never said a word."

Joan swirled her wine in her glass and brought it to her nose for a sniff. "I didn't like what was happening in this room tonight. Krys, have you ever seen the like?"

"Not here," Krystal admitted. "But then, the worst things that have ever happened here were someone stomping off in a dudgeon because they didn't like someone else's opinion."

Harris laughed quietly. "What an image. Well, the truth is, I didn't really suspect someone from here, but…" He turned to Joan. "You bring a new crop of people here every year and have no idea what they might be like. You're not like cops who do background checks."

"No more than a hotel," Joan agreed. "But why should I?"

"Never been a reason before." Harris took another swig of beer.

Krystal had a thought. "You going to call the cops about this, Harris?"

"What good would it do? Reject's an expensive animal, in terms of training and breeding, but what's the sheriff going to do about it? How many deputies can he spare for something like this? Nah, he'll send someone to take a report, maybe look at Reject, and that'll be the end. Besides, I don't want folks getting uneasy 'cuz I brought cops up here to nose around."

"You have a point," Joan said dryly. "God knows how many drugs are floating around Cash Creek Canyon, including here."

Harris smiled. "We got us a funny little town here, don't we? Been funny since the first panners showed up looking for gold. Sometimes I find it hard to believe that was one hundred and sixty years ago. I doubt the place has changed that much, except by shrinking."

"Hard to tell," Joan agreed.

Krystal had to laugh. "Well, there's a gas station…"

The other two grinned. "Got me," Harris said. "Same bank, though."

Now that was hard to believe, Krystal thought. Carrying her brandy glass behind the bar, she began to wash it.

"Leaving already?" Joan asked.

"Bed calls. And I hope I can get some writing done in the morning."

They hugged, then Krystal set out for her cabin with her jacket tightly drawn around her. The rain stung, almost like sleet. Which wouldn't be impossible at this altitude and even in midsummer.

This evening had been quite enough, she thought. The oddness had begun with Josh Healey's unexpected appearance and indirect accusation at lunch, but the evening had grown worse. Far worse.

Something truly ugly had invaded the lodge, however briefly, and it was unnerving. Not her experience of this retreat at all. Not the kind of mood one usually found during an evening gathering.

In fact, that evening's gathering had been larger than usual. A lot of the artists liked to get out for an evening stroll along well-marked paths in the woods. Some had friends they visited in Conard City. Some just drove away for a few hours for a change of scenery. But rarely did it feel as if everyone was in that room at the same time.

Tonight it had. And Krystal had an uncomfortable feeling about the reason. The guests had felt threatened by Healey's visit. They'd instinctively come together like a herd seeking safety. Then the evening had verged not on Paul Bunyan tales but something far uglier.

All started by Mason Cambridge, no doubt. The guy made his living off stories of horrible crimes. Unspeakable acts. Why wouldn't he try to turn Healey's visit into something much darker?

He was going to need some reining in, she thought, but she wasn't sure anyone had ever been able to rein in that man. Bullheaded, pigheaded and egotistical beyond description.

She could almost have believed that Mason had set the whole situation up with the dog just to start a real-life experience of his ugly suspicions of the human race. To entertain himself. Or give himself ideas for a new book.

Then she felt disgusted with herself for harboring such suspicions about anyone, even Mason Cambridge.

No, it hadn't been a good day.

Her cabin still held some of the day's warmth and soon she had a small fire going on her woodstove. Its heat and the glow through the front grating were welcome. She booted her computer and tested her internet connection. Good, the storm, such as it was, hadn't knocked her antenna out of line. Without it, she'd have been lost at sea.

Another way Cash Creek Canyon had changed from the old days: instant connection with the outside world.

Instead of trying to work, however, she began reading articles from some of the science magazines she subscribed to. Interest led her to JSTOR and current research in science publications. By the time she started yawning, she had an idea for an article about some of the recent developments in physics.

Well, she wrote and sold some of those for magazines that catered to lay readers. Another way to put off working on her novel. On the other hand, it would help with her bills.

Satisfied, she washed up, then snuggled into her bed. Only when she turned off the light did she feel the night pressing in.

She didn't feel like that, she thought, annoyed with herself. She never felt the forest as if it were a threat and not a baby's cradle.

But the feeling wouldn't leave her. To her amazement, an image of Josh Healey rose in her mind, and this time she felt only that he was built to be a protector.

Somehow that eased her fears enough to carry her into sleep with one last thought. *God, this is ridiculous!*

JOSH HEALEY SAT in a wooden rocking chair near a fire some of his people had built. They could have had fire inside the refurbished buildings that held fireplaces, but most of them still felt better being in the large, open parade area. Many remained uncomfortable in closed spaces. Hardly surprising given their experiences.

Time within these walls was a deliberately slow and free space. No one got pushed, except gently when necessary. Josh made sure there were always plenty of manual tasks to do, tasks as far away from battle as possible.

They built furniture, like this chair he sat on. When they made enough furniture, he sometimes filled an old box truck with it and carted it to Casper or Laramie to sell. A sense of accomplishment for men and women who had little enough of that.

Flower gardens, well tended. A vegetable garden that might have done better at a lower altitude but was good enough. Repairs around the stockade. There was always work that needed doing.

And of course, there were the group therapy sessions. In answer to his own combat experiences, he'd chosen to become an educated, licensed counselor, simultaneously dealing with his own reentry problems and those of his fellow vets.

Admittedly, he could only help a small group at a time out here, maybe two or three dozen, but getting even these few people away from every possible trigger sure helped.

Inevitably, though, his thoughts turned to that injured dog. To the artists' retreat on the other side of the creek. To the woman who had confronted him.

He kinda liked Krystal's fire. Given his size and his appearance, few people gave him a piece of their minds, but she had. Not afraid of him. A plus.

Still, there were all those people over at the retreat, many of them unknown variables. He gathered some were regular visitors, but what about the rest? Who knew a damn thing about *them*?

He'd learned, too, that those creative types weren't allowed to bring weapons to the retreat. That had been made clear in a magazine ad that had somehow come with his infrequent mail delivery. No weapons of any kind.

What guarantee was there that anyone would listen to that, anyway? He hadn't noticed any metal detectors around the place when he'd gone out on one of his nightly patrols to keep an eye on the surrounding area.

Surreptitious night patrols. Quiet, moving among the shadows as he'd learned to do under hostile conditions. And frankly, he traveled armed with a KA-BAR. He wasn't much worried about encountering an armed hostile human, but there were other things out there, like some large black bears and the grizzly he'd seen once.

He didn't look for a confrontation, but you could never be positive that you wouldn't get between a mama and her cubs. Or just meet an annoyed, territorial grizzly. They didn't always need a reason to attack.

Anyway, he sat on his chair, half listening to the desultory conversation between men and women, some of them edged with the distrust that had its birth in places where you couldn't trust very much except your immediate buddies. None of this group of vets had been his battle buddies except for Angus MacDougall, who'd served twice with Josh. Angus had become a sort of second-in-command inside the compound.

Because there was a reluctance among many to deal with a life that had no laid-out order, some discipline existed. Guidelines to appropriate behavior.

Josh sighed when he considered all the ways a few years in a threatening military environment could affect a soldier. Some simply couldn't give up a sense of order, the one thing they could depend on. Others had taken great pleasure in finding their way around rules, like the military's general order, long since abandoned, that forbade animals to be taken as pets.

Yet, despite minor rebellions, in the service autonomy had nearly disappeared. And Josh had to thread the needle, trying to bring back damaged minds to a place where they could adequately function in a very different world. A world that had been scrubbed from them by training and combat.

Considering that he was trying to protect these vets from a world they couldn't yet handle, he'd probably done a very foolish thing by crossing the creek to tell the people in that damn retreat about the dog. To practically accuse them.

But he'd been angry. More than angry. He'd been furious. The idea that anyone would do this to his vets made him livid. How many may have had their recoveries set back by the implicit threat? It'd be a while before he knew.

But once again his thoughts drifted to Krystal Metcalfe. Easier to think about her than some of the things going on around here.

She owned the retreat with her mother. The magazine ad that had somehow dropped into his mailbox had told him about it. Had painted a truly engaging portrait of the entire Mountain Artists' Retreat. Although why artists needed a retreat left Josh flummoxed.

But the two-page ad had promised private cabins, meals served in a main dining room if you wanted them, a gathering place for those who wanted to exchange ideas. The only restrictions were to bring no weapons and never to bother another guest without an invitation. Apparently no running next door for a cup of sugar.

But that restriction on weapons had caught his attention.

Were the retreat owners worried about violence among their clients? Or was it a simple bid to create a sense of safety in a culture that seemed to be growing less so?

Beat the hell out of him. Anyone who'd seen what an assault weapon could do to a human body would never *want* to fire one again—unless, of course, they'd slipped a cog. He'd known a few of *them*, too.

Shaking his head, he rose from his chair and began to walk around the parade ground inside the stockade. Plenty of room in here, even with the two houses and gardens and work shed. Not too big, not offering enough space to make anyone feel that protection was limited, but big enough to allow free roam to the vets.

Not an easy balance. No one would ever know the years he'd spent planning this. The years of research. Not that it mattered. He'd succeeded as well as any man could.

"Josh." One of his female vets emerged from the relative darkness and strode by with a nod. "Carly," he answered. Carly Narth. It had taken three months to get her past calling him Colonel. A small triumph.

When he reached the wooden steps, he climbed up to the walkway that lined the stockade about four feet below its top. From there he could have a view of the woods around and at least part of the retreat across the creek. He walked slowly again, scanning the world, seeing nothing amiss. Halting finally where he had a clear view of Krystal's cabin. She seemed to have retired for the night.

He gave her props for that. After the dog incident, he didn't feel he could let down his guard in the least.

Which might be an overreaction, but he didn't think so. That dog had been placed there for a reason, and there was always the possibility it was an opening salvo against the stockade and the men and women inside it.

The group of soldiers he both honored and had promised to protect with every ounce of his soul until such time as they were ready to return to the larger world.

A few already had, successfully. A handful more seemed to be verging on recovering as normal a life as they ever could. And a new group would arrive this week, recommended by counselors at Army clinics. Men and women who seemed unable to take the final step into their new world, a world without orders and unending violence. A world where they didn't live with constant threat.

These guys had already won most of his heart. He'd do anything to protect them.

Chapter Four

Morning brought brilliant sunshine, dappled by gently tossing trees, and air that held amazing clarity from the night's light rain. The only sign of the passing wetness was the faint, gray fog beneath the trees, a fog that slowly swallowed the stockade. Above it shone a sky like a blue dome, so bright that it almost hurt to look at it.

While Krystal often skipped breakfast in the lodge so she could sit at her computer and try to work, this morning she decided to follow the path through the woods. To her left the creek ran more quickly and loudly than usual, the gorge filled with the night's gift of water. The steep sides contained it safely, though.

As fresh as the air were the forest scents filling it. Krystal drew deep breath after deep breath, savoring it. Rarely did the world seem as perfect as this. Mother Nature's great gift.

But this morning she was also a bit preoccupied, primarily because she wanted to get a sense of how last night's mood might have shifted. Had uneasiness grown? Or had matters quieted down? What she *didn't* want to do was sit alone at her computer wondering, speculating and creating bad stories of her own.

At least the lodge would offer some distraction. She

hoped. There had been disagreements in the past that had temporarily divided residents, but nothing like this. Overall, the retreat was exactly that: a retreat. People preferred the quiet. Nature. Their privacy in their cabins. When they wanted human company, they arranged it in their own cabins or in the lodge.

One of the other rules at this place was that you didn't go knocking on anyone's door without an invitation. Peace undisturbed. That's why people chose to come here.

But that didn't mean this morning wouldn't be interesting. Not at all. Some minds would be too fired up by yesterday to think about much else.

Krystal smiled wryly. She seemed to have a case of that herself.

Tucked in a heavy-weight blue flannel shirt and jeans with hiking boots, she felt ready for the day. Well, except for her writing. She wondered when she'd ever get around to calling it writer's block. Calling it that seemed so much more important than she could claim.

Maybe her problem was that she didn't feel enough like a writer to call it a block. Laziness, lack of concentration, but nothing as important as a block.

Then her irrepressible sense of humor took over. What did it matter what she called it? Writing a novel was her pipe dream. Helping her mother with the retreat was her *job*. Big difference.

She was smiling as she entered the lodge, but paused on the threshold, surprised by the emptiness of the space. While it was true many of their residents liked to stay in their cabins making coffee and quick breakfasts of their own, there were usually more people here, reading the news on their laptops or tablets. Some making notes of ideas.

This morning there were only four, Mary Collins of the romance writer school, Lars the sculptor, who claimed to have no second name, and Davis Daniels, the graphic artist.

And one more woman, a quiet academic sort who said she was working on her dissertation. Giselle Bibe, that was her name. Preferred to be called Gizzie. Gizzie or Giselle or whatever, with her mousy, lank hair and big dark-rimmed glasses, could have melted into any wall and drawn no attention. Maybe that worked best for the world of academia. Regardless, the single time Krystal had managed to have a conversation with her, she'd proved to have a bright, flexible mind. Even an occasional touch of impish humor.

Krystal hoped they'd have a better chance to grow acquainted, but Gizzie seemed almost entirely buried in her work.

Joan stood propped and sleepy-looking behind the beverage bar as if she were keeping an eye on the coffeepots. Two other employees, both women, hovered around, walking in and out of the kitchen as if waiting for something, anything, to do.

"So, what's up?" Krystal asked Joan.

"Boredom. This place is entirely too empty even for breakfast."

Krystal nodded and pulled a stool over to sit beside her mom. "You look exhausted."

"As if I could sleep last night, thanks to that uproar."

"Mason wasn't any help."

Joan snorted. "Mason is a walking, talking ad for how a normal mind shouldn't work."

Krystal laughed with delight. "Good description."

"I spent most of the night thinking about all of it." Turning a bit, she filled two mugs with coffee and passed one to Krystal. "That dog is really disturbing me, Krys. We've had neighbors take the occasional potshot at one another, but since we, and the Forest Service, got rid of trapping nearly fifty years ago, animals go unharmed around here."

Krystal answered wryly, "So it'd be better if two guys shot at each other over water rights? Grazing rights?"

Joan frowned. "You know exactly what I mean, Krys. This was pointless cruelty. Everyone knows Harris Belcher's sled dogs around here. Never a lick of trouble, unless you want to count that racket those dogs call singing, but Harris is far enough out of town…"

"That it's no big deal," Krystal finished.

Joan shook her head. "You know all this. It's just my mind's been running in circles, mainly about that poor dog."

"And about it being left outside Healey's stockade," Krystal reminded her.

Joan nodded and sipped her coffee, adding a dab more cream to it. "That bothers me, too. Except no one knows a damn thing about any of them inside that stockade."

Krystal sighed and stared at her cup of coffee. Her stomach burned with acid, probably from talking about the dog. Instead, she reached around and grabbed a cruller wrapped in a napkin, hoping it would help. "How many people in our retreat run around announcing their bios to the world? So those soldiers are private. It's their right."

Joan shot her a glance. "Don't tell me you aren't curious. When did you stop wondering? I've heard you."

For once, Krystal didn't mind changing tack. Pulling a

mental U-turn, although she couldn't have said why. "Curiosity is natural. Beyond that it gets sick."

Joan bridled. "Sick?"

"Yeah, Mom. As in rumormongering. As in creating a horror story in here last night, all of it aimed against a group who have done not one bad thing around here." The cruller at least tasted good. She wiped crumbs from her chin.

Joan chewed her lip, then laughed quietly, without any real humor. "You're right, but wasn't it fun?"

Krystal's answer was sour. "Count on Mason Cambridge to start weaving a story that could result in a dangerous mob."

Joan shook her head. "He couldn't do that. Not with all these nice people."

"I have a slightly more jaundiced view of the human race." Which was hardly surprising since she hadn't spent her entire life in these parts and even had a broken heart to show for it. No, she'd gone off to college, a real eye-opener. "Anyway, I'll ask you again. Why do we keep letting that blowhard come here? For him it's just a giant ego stroke to get all those women hanging on his every word."

"Publicity for us."

"Yeah, right. Then people leave here and say bad things about him and by extension about us."

Joan shook her head. "What got into you this morning?"

The same thing that had kept her mother up during the night. The thought of a dog being brutally attacked. The thought of the poor, suffering thing being left outside the stockade where it might well have died in agony before being found. Left like a message, like a piece of trash.

Which led her to the question: Why? Who out there would have it in that much for Josh Healey's group?

Bright sunlight notwithstanding, Krystal felt a shiver of apprehension.

Then, turning her back to her mother, she reached for the landline and called the Conard County Sheriff's Office. Harris Belcher might think it was a waste of time, but Krystal refused to ignore what had happened to that dog.

Someone in this community needed to be scared into behaving or else discover the risk of a jail cell.

If there was one thing Krystal knew about most people in Cash Creek Canyon, they valued the life of any working animal.

So who were the rest?

In the stockade, the morning group therapy ended, followed by a breakfast of homemade bread, orange juice and fried eggs. Everything was prepared by the residents except the juice.

Then everyone, man and woman, scattered around to follow their own pursuits. Some were fond of making furniture. Cleary Howe worked on the plumbing endlessly, slowly bringing hot water to every room in the original house and the scattered outdoor facilities.

Janice Howe, Cleary's wife, took over the garden, sometimes giving orders about hoeing and weeding and fertilizing to anyone who appeared to be just standing around. Around Janice, few stood around.

Elaine Ingall ran a kitchen where they were beginning to put up preserves from the fruit Josh and Angus, Josh's right-hand man, brought back from town by the truckload.

Some of the preserves would probably sell at the county

fair. Some of the wooden furniture that was beginning to
fill the house would also face the same future.

There wasn't a soul in the compound who didn't take
pride in helping the group to be self-supporting. Useful,
whatever their other limitations.

But they still suffered from nightmares that tore the
night wide open. There were still bouts of loss of self-
control, not always caused by anything anyone else could
know. There were nights, and some days, when all that
would help was staying close, offering comfort, letting the
man or woman ride out the horror that memory spewed.
On those days a lot of labor stopped as other vets got triggered or hung on to sanity for dear life.

Yet through it all, Josh saw improvement. Maybe only
in small increments, but improvement just the same.

The incident with the dog hadn't helped anyone. Josh
should have found it on his night patrol, but instead Marvin Damm had snuck out for some reason. Residents were
supposed to stay inside at night because the night often
brought out their biggest fears, their worst memories. Josh
believed it best that none of them was left alone in the dark
hours unless they chose the isolation themselves.

But Marvin had gone out and almost stepped onto the
shivering, wounded animal that lay right outside the small
door.

God! Now Marvin was half a wreck, and nobody in the
compound was doing all that well. They all had memories from the military of animals that had been badly injured. Some had been able to endure the general command
order to leave the animals be. Others had not. Pet dogs
had wound up being concealed in barracks by men and
women who found comfort and pleasure in them.

Now they faced an ugly, familiar situation beyond walls that were supposed to keep them safe while they dealt with their demons. A dog had been shot in the hip.

Wonderful.

Finally, overwhelmed by a need to do something simply because he wasn't by nature able to ignore much, Josh loaded himself into the massive Humvee that usually could get them over the worst roads in the worst conditions and set out for the sled dog operation. He wanted to see for himself how that husky was doing. He hoped to be able to carry back some good news to his group.

The road was decent, once he got past the narrow gravel stretch that led to the stockade. Twenty years of abandonment meant the county hadn't spent a dime on road maintenance. At least he'd been able to pay the power company to hook them up again.

As for the road, once he turned out of his property, he found buckled blacktop that had seen better years.

He knew his way to the sled dog operation run by Harris Belcher and his few mushers. The kennels were rarely quiet, and as Harris had explained when Josh had brought Reject to him yesterday, huskies were talkers. Seldom quiet, holding conversations of their own.

Quite different from the quiet Josh had grown accustomed to in his stockade.

Harris Belcher greeted him warmly enough. "Bet you're here to check on Reject. He's actually doing pretty good, but he just became a house dog."

Josh arched a brow. "House dog?"

"His cast." Harris nodded. "Can't be out getting it wet. But to tell you the truth, I think he's enjoying life in front of a warm fire on a soft rug. Spoiled forever now, probably. Jenine, my secretary, isn't helping much."

Josh smiled, as he rarely did. "You sure he won't want to get back on the trail?"

"Hah!" Harris said. "Damn dog is named Reject for a reason. Never been too cooperative in harness. When he was little more than a pup, I thought he was going to make a great lead. Then he changed his mind and wouldn't change it back. Sometimes I wonder if he just hates having all those other dogs behind him."

Josh's smile widened. "I can identify with that."

Harris eyed him up and down. "Reckon you can."

Just then they both heard the grinding of an engine and the crunch of wheels outside.

"Can't be the vet," Harris remarked. "No need." Then he pulled a ragged curtain back. "Krystal Metcalfe, of all folks. Guess Reject has his own fan club."

"After last night," Josh agreed. But he stiffened anyway, wondering why Krystal should be here when she could have just made a phone call. *Most* phones did work out here.

She slipped a bit on damp pine needles as she approached. Harris threw the door open.

"Girl, what you doing here? You coulda called, which I'm pretty sure Joan would have preferred. Reject's doing pretty good."

Krystal unzipped her jacket, revealing a blue flannel shirt, and looked at both men. "Thought I should give you a personal heads-up. I called the sheriff about Reject and he's going to want to talk with both of you." She eyed Josh. "Good thing you're here because I couldn't get a word out of your compound. Wouldn't want the sheriff banging on the door there, would you?"

No, he wouldn't. He didn't need his people getting unnerved by a noisy—and it would be noisy—bunch of deputies banging at the gate. But before he could speak his objection, Harris beat him to the punch.

"If I'd wanted the sheriff I would have called him, Krystal. Like I said last night, they aren't going to be able to do a damn thing. One dog. A dozen or more residents out here with guns. How much time and effort do you think they're going to spend? Waste of resources."

Krystal's chin set stubbornly. "Never. Maybe making a point that this is illegal will make someone else give it a second thought before using another one of your dogs for target practice."

Just then, Reject hobbled out the door of Harris's cabin and pressed himself to Krystal's leg. She bent and scratched him behind the ears.

After a noticeable pause, Harris said, "Looks like you two have just been invited to coffee."

Josh felt more awkward than he liked to admit. It had been a while since he'd been a guest in someone's house, an ordinary house occupied by ordinary people. He should have turned and left, making some lousy excuse, but a remnant of courtesy held him back.

Like it or not, he was soon sitting at a handcrafted wooden table with two other people, total strangers, and a coffee mug in front of him. Along with a plate of small pastries that looked as if they'd been around for a while. He helped himself anyway. Grub of any kind was always welcome.

Krystal addressed the issue first. "I still can't believe

anyone would treat a dog that way. You say someone must have removed him from the kennel?"

"Yup."

Reject took that moment to curl as best he could around Krystal's feet. Ignoring her coffee and the dubious pastries, she bent and began to pet him. "Poor baby. Are you going to be okay?"

Harris's face darkened. "Lame. He's going to be lame. But nobody could have hurt him like that unless they managed to pull him out of his run. Damn dog could have leaped any one of those fences like lightning. Danged if I can figure how anybody managed to catch him."

Continuing to pet Reject, Krystal raised her head enough to eye Harris. "Then how do you keep these dogs from scattering all over hell and gone?"

Harris sighed and raised one shoulder. "Huskies are interesting dogs, Krys. They listen as much as they choose. They like sledding, they like the communal nature of the big yard and the runs. If they didn't like it, they'd be gone. But another thing."

Krystal nodded. "Yes?"

"They get attached just like we get attached to them. Can't keep any husky that wants to run, but a lot of them choose to stay. You'd have to ask them the difference."

"Loyalty," Krystal suggested.

"I sometimes wonder. I ever tell you about one of my mushers?"

"Which one?"

Now Harris grinned and shook his head at the same time. "Aaron he was. One of the best. He was training his team and some backups for the Iditarod. Anyway, every single day he'd take them out for a good run with a loaded sled. Tires instead of runners unless there was snow."

"And?" Josh asked.

"Well, now, that got interesting. His team went absolutely nuts somewhere along the trail. You got to understand something about these dogs. They behave until they sense trouble. Saved more than one musher from serious harm by refusing to go over a river that wasn't frozen enough or down a gully that was steep enough to break a neck. They won't go into trouble and won't take their musher into it even when ordered. Smart buggers."

Krystal found herself waiting almost breathlessly. "What happened?"

"Aaron's team came running back here, hell-for-leather, harnesses snapped or jerked out of. Every single dog except one."

"That's a problem," Josh remarked. "Always trouble when a team comes back missing a dog."

Harris nodded. "You got it. So we gathered another team, well rested, and took them out to follow Aaron's trail. They'd find him, for sure."

Harris slugged more coffee. "They found him, all right. Went nuts. We managed to keep them on harness, but they kept yanking to go back home. We knew damn well something had happened there. Finally, handling the team and trying to hunt for Aaron was too much. We let them run home and started bellowing into the woods."

Krystal was now on the edge of her seat. "Aaron? What happened with Aaron?"

"Maybe I should tell you that bears and huskies are sworn enemies. A husky will take off like greased lightning from a bear, and bears hate the dogs just as much. Wanna kill 'em."

Harris shook his head. "Long story short. We heard Aaron call out and found the damnedest thing. He was most the way up a tree, bleeding from a swipe at his hip, and his lead dog was at the foot of the tree, snarling and barking at a damn bear. Don't ask me how that dog survived, or why the bear kept backing off. Six hours of that, Aaron said. Anyway, we made a lot of gunfire to scare the bear off and get Aaron down. He was okay but he was done with sledding."

Josh leaned forward. "Wasn't that unusual behavior for the bear?"

"Yeah. Unusual for the dog, too. Loyalty. Anyway, Cannon, the dog's name, died a couple of years later. Got a hero's funeral here. Not many like him."

Krystal looked down at the dog now sleeping at her feet. "What happens to Reject now, if he's lame?"

"Somebody's house pet, if he doesn't skedaddle on them."

Krystal hesitated only a moment. "Do you think he'd come with me?"

"Do you think those fool clients of yours would tolerate him?"

Krystal felt an instant of rebellion. "I don't give a damn."

Surprising her, Josh Healey laughed. "Go, lady, go. You gotta have *something* the way you want it."

She bridled. This man made her want to fight for some reason. "How would you know what I have?"

He shrugged a shoulder, but his smile never quite faded. "Something about you."

For some reason, Krystal felt as if those strangely intense aquamarine eyes of his had just stripped her emotionally naked. She didn't like the feeling at all and immediately stood.

"Thanks for the coffee, Harris," she said. "I've gotta run. Just keep me posted about Reject. Trust me, I'd like to have him."

"If he climbs in that truck of yours with you, then he's made up his own mind."

JOSH LINGERED A bit longer, thinking the matter over, deflecting some of Harris's questions about the stockade, but doing so carefully. He didn't want to feed the curiosity around here in a way that would be dangerous to his soldiers.

"You know," Josh said presently, "I have some folks who'd love a puppy or two as well."

Harris eyed him closely. "How can you be sure of that?"

"Because I saw them with strays over there in combat zones. I saw them rescue dogs in defiance of general orders. Some worked every angle they could to try to get a dog home with them."

Harris nodded slowly. "I've got a new litter of five. I don't separate them until the bitch weans 'em herself. Maybe four weeks more."

"That's good, not weaning them early."

Now it was Harris's turn to smile. "Guess you know something after all."

Then the crunch of tires on the gravel drew both men's attention.

Harris cussed. "That'll be the sheriff. Why the hell did Krys have to call him? Not gonna do a damn thing about this, I swear."

KRYSTAL WASN'T FAR behind the sheriff's vehicle. As soon as she saw it passing uphill toward the sledding ranch, she pulled a U-turn and followed. Harris had been so dubious about help, she wanted to hear the conversation for herself.

She stopped right behind the official vehicle and climbed out. Josh's Humvee was still here, too, which kind of surprised her. She'd expected him to follow her down the hill within minutes. Of course, where would he have gone that she wouldn't have passed him, too?

Dang, was she scattering all her marbles around here? The obvious sometimes escaped her. Maybe it was time to visit Conard City and her friends there. Fresh concerns, fresh topics of conversation. A livelier world. One that might actually wake her up.

The officer who stepped out of the official Suburban surprised her, however. It was the sheriff himself, Gage Dalton, a man with a long history around these parts who commanded a whole lot of respect. Given his old injuries, however, Krystal was more used to seeing him behind a desk.

He limped when he walked, wasn't always able to conceal a wince when he moved, and one side of his face bore the shiny skin of a bad burn in his past.

He turned as he saw her and gave her his patented half smile, all his scarred face would still let him do. "Riding shotgun, Krystal?"

"Curious, more like. Mind?"

Dalton shook his head as he clapped his tan uniform Stetson on it. "Public service and all that."

She arched a brow and laughed. "Right. All public until you need to keep secrets."

"About investigations in progress? You got that right."

They were now side by side, heading for Harris's porch when the door opened.

"Crap," said Harris succinctly. "What are you gonna do about one dog, Gage? Like you don't have enough to do keeping a lid on this entire county? But get your butt in here. I seem to be having a meeting."

Josh was still at the table, a mug in front of him. Harris, rather gracelessly, ordered them all to chairs, then brought out another plate of pastries, saying, "Well, these are fresh, anyway."

Krystal couldn't suppress a laugh. "I'm heading into Conard City later. I'll get you some fresh from Melinda."

"Good, because I don't get there often."

Which was true, Krystal thought as Harris freshened her mug and poured a coffee for Gage. Then he faced the three of them before boring his gaze into Gage.

"So, Sheriff, what the hell you gonna do and why should you even want to bother?"

Gage leaned back in his chair, wincing a bit but otherwise concealing his discomfort. "Interesting question, Harris. Why should I give a damn about a dog, huh?"

Harris shifted unhappily. "I didn't say it that way. Not exactly."

"But that's what you're thinking. And that's why I'm here instead of one of my deputies."

Harris shook his head. "So tell me."

"Because," Gage said quietly, "I got a hang-up about people who torture animals. And from what Mike Windwalker, the vet, told me, this was torture. Not meant to kill, not even the shooting."

Krystal drew a deep breath. Harris's face darkened like a thundercloud. "No," he said after a few beats.

"I'm sure you hate it, too," Gage continued, now reaching for his coffee and taking a sip. "Damn, Harris, I think you've got Velma beat in the lousy coffee category."

At that Harris delivered a reluctant smile. Velma was the sheriff's chief dispatcher, and her coffee was infamous. "Took lessons, Gage."

"You might give her some yourself." Gage put the mug down and looked at both Krystal and Josh. "You found the dog, Josh, right?"

Josh nodded. "Well, one of my people did. Gave him what first aid we could and brought him up here."

Gage nodded again, pulling a small notebook from his pocket and scanning it quickly. "Says here about two a.m."

"About that. Close enough."

Then Gage turned his attention to Harris. "Your dogs found where the attack happened?"

Harris nodded. "Right after the vet left around three yesterday morning. The dogs were going bonkers, Gage. They knew. So I let out a team of them and they took off hell-for-leather. Found the place where there was blood."

"You gonna show me?" Gage asked.

"Hell yeah, much good it'll do. Dogs been all over it."

"Maybe a lot of *people* haven't. I've got a couple of good trackers. I'll bring them up."

Harris snorted. "Won't find much. Somehow these bastards got Reject down to the stockade and I didn't see a trail of any kind."

"You never know." Gage reached for his mug again, then thought better of it. Instead he took a pastry. "Okay, Harris, I got another concern than just Reject."

Harris's face tightened, but he nodded.

"I'm furious that anyone would treat an animal that

way, but there's another issue here. If someone would do that to your dog, they're dangerous to people, too. You follow me?"

Krystal felt her face drain. She hadn't thought of that. Beside her, Josh stiffened.

"Takes a certain kind," Gage said, pushing back his chair. "I'm not going to let this go just because of Reject, Harris. I'm also not going to let it go because of people. You could say this creep just unleashed a two-edged sword. We aren't going to stop."

Soon three vehicles made their way down the slope toward the retreat and the stockade. Toward Cash Creek Canyon, such as it was. Beside Krystal on the bench seat of her truck, Reject lay curled up. Apparently he'd made his decision.

Harris's road was in great shape, thanks to the business he brought. Lots of folks evidently liked the idea of mushing through the winter woods and sleeping in yurts covered with snow.

Nobody in their right mind, Krystal privately thought. Oh, she loved sledding with one of Harris's teams for a day, but for a weekend? Or a week? That much cold didn't appeal to her. Too many winters up here, she supposed.

To her surprise, Josh followed her down her narrow driveway to her cabin. Now, what was she supposed to do about that? She didn't know him well enough to invite him inside, but she didn't want to be rude either.

When he climbed out of his Humvee, however, he stared across the creek at his stockade and didn't at all look like a man who expected any kind of invitation. When he spoke, his direction surprised her.

"Gage unnerved you?" he asked.

She hesitated, wanting to be honest but not sound like a wimp either. "Not completely," she said after a bit.

"Yeah."

Wondering where this all might be leading, Krystal climbed her two porch steps and sat in her favorite Adirondack chair. Then, after the briefest hesitation, she motioned Josh to one of the others. Surprising her, totally out of character from what she'd seen of him, he accepted the invitation, sitting with one ankle on the other knee. A perennial masculine pose. Shrugging, she put her feet up on the railing. Beyond that, she offered no hospitality.

"I suppose," he said presently, "that you have no idea what we're doing across the creek."

"You hardly advertise," she said dryly.

"No. That's on purpose. But given this development, you should know."

She turned her head, curiosity awakening in her. "How so?"

"If anything more happens around here, we're apt to be blamed for it."

Now she pushed forward, sitting up straight. "Why on God's earth…?"

He passed his hand over his face. "Because we're vets. Every damn one of us. You know what some people say."

Krystal drew a deep breath, her hands tightening. "I know what *some* people say. And most of it isn't true."

"Then that makes you a majority of one."

She thought she detected a bitter note in his voice. "But why do you all have to stay over there? Are any of you afraid of what you might do?"

"Goddamn," he swore, sitting bolt upright. "You know,

it never occurs to anyone that those walls might have been built to keep the rest of the world out, not to keep *us* in."

Krystal felt slammed as her world tilted in an entirely new direction. No, she hadn't thought of it that way. Not at all.

Josh stood, evidently having had enough of his attempt to be sociable. Krystal felt just awful and jumped to her own feet.

"Josh, I'm sorry…"

"Why?" he asked bluntly. "You're no different from the rest."

Then he strode to his Humvee and took off with a pointed scatter of gravel.

Great, Krystal thought, watching him disappear into the woods along the winding road. This was a guy who'd saved a wounded dog and then she'd hinted at the general view of vets as a threat.

God!

And she'd blown her one chance to get to know the man better. She seriously doubted she'd get another one.

Totally annoyed with herself, she went inside her cabin and switched on her computer. As soon as it booted itself, she turned it off again.

Screw that. Climbing into warmer gear, she grabbed her rumpled pack and headed up the trail to the lodge. Reject limped beside her. Now would not be a good time to be alone.

BACK AT HIS COMPOUND, Josh found his crew considerably quieter than they'd been since they found the dog. Most of them had picked up their regular chores. Those who hadn't sat clumped together, trying to talk in spurts about feelings that didn't lend themselves to words.

He wondered how much the ugly incident had set some of them back. Didn't know exactly how he was going to deal with it. Maybe this was one of those things that would take the entire group.

He found plenty of coffee in the urn and poured himself one of those tall, insulated mugs with a dash of cream. Cream was still a luxury to him.

Then he sat on his usual wood chair in the big room, waiting for the circle to gather. He wondered how many would show, especially since this wasn't the usual time for group. Slowly, however, most of the gang gathered.

For a long time, no one said anything. Silence in this group of men and women often spoke more than words might.

It was Marvin Damm, who'd found the dog the night before last, who spoke first. "Did it live?"

Eyes focused on Josh.

"Yes," he said. "He's going to be lame, but he'll be fine. I guess the woman across the creek is adopting him." He paused, then added, "The dog's name is Reject."

A few people swore, one man and two women.

"Who the hell names a dog that? Damn it," Carly added angrily, *"we're all rejects."*

Angus MacDougall, who'd become a version of Josh's second hand, spoke. "Ain't none of us *rejects*. Need to remember who rejected who."

Josh nodded, agreeing wholeheartedly and glad Angus had spoken the words, his Scottish burr seeming to add them weight.

"But why *Reject*?" Carly Narth asked. A roadside bomb had left her with a scarred face and patchy gray hair.

"Simple," Josh answered, glad he'd learned this much. "Harris thought he was going to make a great team lead when he was a pup, but then Reject changed his mind about that. Question is who did the rejecting."

That at least brought out a few weak laughs. A couple of the guys gave each other playful shoves. Tension eased from the room.

But Josh knew he couldn't leave it there. It was too important to leave there. But how he hated to give these people another reason for concern.

"There's more," he finally said. Once again all attention fixed on him. "The sheriff is concerned that this could be…something more headed our way. As in someone who might start maiming *people*."

This time there was no silence. A cacophony rose in the room nearly deafening in its intensity. Josh let it run, let the energy burn out as it needed to. There'd come a point when fury and despair would give way to other feelings. None of them good, of that he was certain.

But eventually the noise quieted. A few cusses and nasty remarks escaped, then everyone fell silent. Except for Elaine, their head cook.

"Let me guess," she said bitterly. "They're blaming *us*."

"Nobody's blaming anyone." Which was true insofar as Josh knew. "Not yet, anyway."

Marvin Damm stood up, knocking his chair over. "They'll get around to it," he said, anger creeping back into his voice and posture. "There isn't a one of us in this room that hasn't been picked up by cops for questioning the instant something bad happens."

Grumbles of agreement answered him.

Josh tried to conceal his own growing stress, even though he knew this group was right. All of them. Even himself with his bloody degree and years of training. Easy targets, vets who couldn't readjust. Who had gotten thrown out by their families, who wound up living on the streets because there was nothing for them at a VA hospital except a cup of pills that didn't always work.

Homeless. Unwanted. Until a crime occurred. Then once they'd been picked up for questioning, for any reason, they were on a list for investigation for the next crime. Innocence meant nothing to the law.

There were a couple of former MPs in this group, and they knew the mindset all too well. They dinned a frequent warning about leaving the stockade, especially alone.

Now this.

"Serial killers du jour," one of the former MPs said. Rusty Rodes.

The problem was that Rusty wasn't far from correct.

Chapter Five

Krystal found the lodge busier than it had been that morning. The lunch crowd beginning to gather?

Then she saw the look on her mother's face as she supervised the kitchen help in preparing the buffet luncheon. Krystal went to her immediately. "What's up?"

Joan jerked her head toward the large windows where sunshine spilled into the room, a direct contrast to last night. And there she saw Mason Cambridge, once again holding court, although this time more quietly.

Krystal sighed. "You sure we can't ban him?"

"The idea grows stronger every day. But I've told you…"

"Yeah." Krystal sighed again. "It doesn't help that he gives a seminar every year. More publicity."

Joan cocked an eye at her daughter. "I have no idea how useful many of those seminars are."

Krystal shrugged. "People keep signing up for them."

"Unfortunately. Oh, we're getting a new guest today."

Krystal turned to her. "Do we have room?"

"That empty cottage next to Mason's, the one he insists on renting for the sake of privacy. Anyway, his agent is arriving this afternoon."

Krystal could have snickered. "Poor woman." Darlene

Dana, who had been Mason's agent since he was discovered, never failed to look harassed, exasperated and fatigued after a few days with her star client. Krystal didn't envy the woman her job no matter how much it might pay.

"Yeah, poor her," Joan agreed. "Except she *could* kick him to the curb. God knows, I'm tempted."

"So what's he on about today?"

"Maimed dogs, things that creep in the night. He's working up to some real bonfire-type scares tonight."

"Maybe we should light a fire outside and give him free rein." The look on Joan's face succeeded in making Krystal laugh.

At that opportune moment, Davis Daniels showed up, heading straight for the buffet, where Joan and Krystal stood. "Let me guess," he said without preamble. "Our star egotist is setting up a good scare for later. By the time he's done we'll have Michael what's-his-name out there in the trees."

"That ought to keep everyone safely inside," Joan remarked tartly. "No wondering if someone out there stepped off a path and sprained an ankle."

Davis filled a plate with eggs, bacon and pastry, but took a seat at the end of the bar, rather than a table. "You know, Joan, this is a quiet place. I love coming here every year. For a little while I can turn off the world and focus on my art. It doesn't even have to be comic art unless I have a contract. For a little while I can remember the joy that brought me into this field."

"That's really special," Krystal said enviously.

Davis eyed her. "And you can't, at least not right now. Here's an idea. Unless Joan objects, why don't you come with me on a hike up Morris Trail?"

Morris Trail was one of the most difficult hikes around the property. "Takes a lot of energy," she remarked.

"Exactly." Davis's eyes twinkled. "I'm telling you, there's nothing like working your body hard to free your mind."

Krystal found the idea appealing, even though she knew that Morris Trail was apt to leave her dead on her feet by the time they returned. "You're on."

Joan smiled. "Good. It'll get you out of here and doing something refreshing for a while."

Which was how the next morning Krystal came to be wearing a small backpack containing water bottles and rain gear, all the items necessary for safety in a mountain climb where the weather could suddenly change. She followed Davis up the steep, rough incline.

"It'll be easier on the way down," he said over his shoulder.

As if she didn't know. "I'll be too damn tired to care."

He laughed, the sound ringing through the woods.

But halfway up the three-mile climb, the wind shifted and its odor changed, stinging with sharp ozone.

"Davis," she called out.

He, too, had paused and tipped his head up. "End of hiking today," he agreed. "Grab your rain gear."

"Again," she said disbelievingly. Rain, on this side of the mountains, was rare enough to create a wonderful climate for their guests to enjoy. They'd just had that light rain, and now something that looked as if it might become bad. But surely it would blow over because of the updraft against the mountains?

Just then, she thought she heard a buzz in the air.

"Hell," Davis said, just as she recognized the sound.

A charge was building in the air around them. Lightning. Her hair started to stand up. Krystal needed no directions. She dropped low, grabbing her ankles, tucking her head, hoping Davis did the same. There was no time to fool around, not now. Not even to give one another directions.

It seemed like an eternity later that the buzzing eased up, then there was a blinding flash and a deafening crack in the same instant.

But the buzzing remained gone.

She and Davis rose quickly to see a nearby tree smoking. Without another word, they headed back down the mountain as fast as their feet would carry them.

Well, this would make a good story, Krystal thought a bit crazily, not sure if she was more frightened or more relieved. It might even silence Mason.

At the foot of the trail, the lodge was only twenty feet away. Rain had begun to patter lightly and more loud thunder rolled down the mountain. Not until she and Davis were inside did she feel fully safe.

"Thank God," Joan said as soon as she saw them. "I was so scared when that storm broke."

Davis replied, "Not as scared as we were. We just missed getting zapped."

The silence from Mason's table became huge as the group heard Davis. Krystal decided to enjoy it. Maybe there was an upside to being almost fried.

Joan reached out and touched her arm. "Honey?"

Krystal worked up a smile. "I'm okay, really. We didn't have much time to get frightened, did we, Davis."

He twisted his mouth. "Unless you count the fastest run down Morris Trail ever recorded."

With that wry comment, Krystal relaxed completely. Davis, too, looked contented enough and Mason's coterie went back to talking esoterically about writing. Although Krystal was of the opinion that there was nothing at all esoteric about writing. At least not his.

"Not going back to work today, honey?" Joan asked, still looking a bit concerned.

"The lightning didn't kick my brain into high gear."

Just then, along with the freshening breeze and the growing smell of ozone, the front door opened and a woman appeared, looking only slightly ruffled by the wind outdoors. Along with her came the boom of thunder. A perfect entrance, Krystal thought, unable to suppress unexpected amusement.

Darlene Dana, Mason's agent, always looked as if she had stepped off a page of *Vogue*, even as the wind tossed her long auburn hair around. That look wouldn't last long, however. Darlene wasn't above dressing down for the situation. Soon she'd be wearing casual slacks and a T-shirt or sweatshirt.

Right now, though, she made every other woman in the room look or feel dull.

But Darlene smiled her thousand-watt smile at everyone, waving to Joan and Krystal, then heading in a straight line for Mason's table.

Mason might try to worm out of it with an early drink, but Krystal had seen how well Darlene could pretend a friendly conversation while keeping the through line on Mason's next book. Watching Mason holding court, Krystal sometimes wondered how he ever completed a book at all.

Or why his publisher offered him bonuses just for being almost on time.

And one of those bonuses seemed to be a visit from Darlene.

As usual, Mason spent some time with his followers, no doubt impressing them with his importance in having his agent visit him. Then, with a promise to see them all that evening, he marched off with Darlene into the building storm.

"I suppose," Joan said as they disappeared, "I should have warned them how bad it is."

Davis shook his head. "He heard Krys and me talk about it. If he hasn't the sense to stay in here, then he gets what he might deserve."

"But what about Darlene?" Krystal asked.

Davis laughed. "She probably has the sense to duck."

Thunder rumbled again, as if joining the conversation, but it didn't sound as close as it had earlier.

In ones and twos other guests began to wander in, looking for lunch ostensibly, but likely not wanting to be in their cabins alone for nature's display. If it got loud enough, Krystal knew, it could be hard to concentrate on anything else. It could also be unnerving the way the mountains seemed to amplify the sound and bounce it back and forth like a hard rubber ball.

Washington Irving, she thought. Rip Van Winkle, the bowling gnomes under the mountain. She could understand where that story had been born.

Which brought her to "The Legend of Sleepy Hollow." Irving's tale had been more frightening than the movie, but beyond the windows the day had begun to darken as if night approached, and this night wasn't quieting early.

Joan had already signaled the staff to start building fires in the two large fireplaces. Sizable cast-iron cooking pots waited nearby in case they lost power. Out back a generator stood ready if needed, and Krystal merely shook her head, dreading its use. The lodge's generator beat the vets' hands down when it came to noise, even though Joan had arranged for it to be built into the ground.

All ready, Krystal thought, looking around as the room filled up. Only Mason and his agent were absent, not necessarily a bad thing. Whatever the two of them discussed had always remained private, unlike Mason's endless tales of what it meant to be a published author, what it took to succeed and why he had a gift few else could hope for.

Although Krystal thought rather sarcastically that Mason's success had been bought in part by knowing the right people in the industry.

Oh, man, she thought suddenly. Was she turning into an ugly, vindictive person? Not even Mason deserved such unkind thoughts from her.

Seeking distraction from herself, she turned to helping the staff fill up the food buffet. Mealtime or not, it didn't take long for folks to start seeking the comfort of food.

And beyond the windows the afternoon continued to darken threateningly. Along with it, quantities of carbs began to disappear from the buffet. Cookies, fried potatoes, cakes. Rolls, buttered bread…hell, all the serotonin fuelers.

Now, that was amusing and improved Krystal's mood considerably. She even joined in the fun with a giant cinnamon roll.

The day continued to darken. The thunder grew louder. Reject wandered around, appearing disinterested.

And suddenly out of nowhere, Krystal thought of the vets down in Josh's compound. This must be god-awful for them, the endless rolling of the noises of war.

DOWN BELOW IN the stockade, the place of safety that Josh and his vets had built, the storm was making matters less safe for each and every one of them. The rolling thunder began to come too frequently, sounding like a determined barrage. The echo off the mountains added to the sense of surrounding danger. Men and women, knowing consciously that they were now safe from the war, nonetheless began to group into knots.

Hell, Josh thought. Hell, hell, hell. He wondered how much hard work was being undone by one overwhelming storm. Past storms had been easier to tolerate, being quieter, less reminiscent of threats of death. This storm embodied the worst.

Then, like a small ray of light in the midst of a nightmare, Angus called out. Angus was the man Josh could rely on no matter what.

"I think that dog is back again."

It was Josh who went out to check, asking no one else to step outside these protective walls, such as they were.

It was indeed the dog they had rescued just the other day. How the hell had he gotten over here on that leg?

This time, however, instead of looking sickly and hurt, the animal seemed determined to get attention. And it wasn't friendly attention, Josh realized, as the husky once again moved away each time he held out his hands.

Turning, he called back through the partly opened door. "Angus? Call that sledding guy. It's his wounded animal."

"Dang, won't the damn thing come in out of the storm? And I thought that woman adopted him."

"Maybe not. Maybe that guy, Harris, I think he is, can come down and get him."

Angus snorted. "Like anyone's going to come out into this crap weather."

Josh had his doubts about that, too, but this dog meant something to Harris, and Josh wasn't going to let the dog suffer needlessly. It went against every bone in his body.

So he stood there, water dripping off his camouflage poncho like a waterfall, and stared at a stubborn dog who was apt to freeze to death if he didn't get warm soon.

And that leg! Mike Windwalker, the vet, had put screws and plates in one of them in the wee hours, then splinted both of them, and now the protective cast on one was getting soaked and probably liable to infection.

"Stupid mutt," Josh muttered. Except nothing about that dog felt stupid right then. Reject bore a message of some kind. He'd known dogs like that in the K-9 Corps. Smart. Never to be diverted from anything it considered to be a duty.

Just as he was getting fed up—he didn't know what to do about it if that dog kept dancing away—Angus stuck his head out. "Phone's out to the sled dog place."

"Sat phone, too?"

"Hell yeah, and you ain't gonna get anyone on the roof to adjust the dish."

Not in the middle of this storm. No way. That left one option. "Call the lodge and tell 'em I'm on the way. Maybe they still got a phone."

Angus's voice became sarcastic. "And just how you supposin' to get that damn animal in the car?"

Josh was past caring. The dog had ridden in the Humvee before. No reason he should refuse today. If he did, Josh couldn't even get his owner down here to help.

So be it.

But Reject had a plan of his own, and it involved struggling his way into the vehicle. This time he even let Josh help him.

Crazy dog.

THE THUNDER HAD grown particularly bad by the time Krystal heard the muffled growl of a vehicle pulling up out front. While everyone else in the lodge remained occupied with card games or conversations, she went to the door and looked. The wide porch roof provided some shelter from the storm.

Krystal immediately recognized the Humvee. What had brought him up here? The hermit and his band of nearly invisible recluses from below seemed unlikely visitors.

But as soon as he opened his vehicle door, she saw Reject leap out and run limping through the lodge door into the great room.

She looked at Josh, who now stood there on the porch in his dripping camouflage poncho, and saw him shrug. "Don't ask me. He wouldn't settle for anything else."

Krystal turned to look at Reject limping across the room to the big windows. "I hope he didn't hurt himself. And I don't get why he left the lodge."

Josh just shook his head. "Like anyone tells that dog what to do. Anyway, my phone is down, including the sat lines. So I thought maybe you can still get through to

Harris, in case Reject damaged his cast, maybe on your landline."

"Well, come on in and we can check. Dry off. Eat. Have coffee. We seem to have become food and drink central today."

He chuckled quietly. "I can get that. My people don't want to be out in this either."

"So that leaves Reject."

Josh stepped inside and shed his poncho, hanging it on a hook with a bunch of other rain gear. "My boots are muddy."

"Join the crowd." But he scuffed his boots on the big entrance mat anyway, removing what he could.

Since he was a stranger to most of the artists in residence, he got only the merest greetings, but no one was impolite. Davis Daniels, the digital artist, greeted him warmest of all and patted the bar stool beside him. "What's with the dog?"

Josh slid onto the stool. "You'll have to ask him. Joan? Did you get through to the sled dog place?"

Joan shook her head, laying the satellite phone on the counter. "Nothing. No landline, no cell, no sat phone. Well and truly cut off."

It wasn't the first time the retreat had experienced this kind of electronic failure, but for the very first time it made Krystal uneasy. She looked from Josh to Davis to her mother and felt no better when she saw a tightness around their eyes. They felt it, too.

Then she looked at the clearly stubborn Reject, who was sitting near the windows. "I guess we don't need to call Harris, anyway. He's supposed to be *my* dog now."

"I was concerned about his cast," Josh said, "but honestly, it doesn't seem to have gotten too messed up."

Instinctively, however, Krystal looked toward the tall windows again, more intently, where Reject had planted himself. "Maybe we should cover the windows." She couldn't have explained her uneasiness even to herself, but watching Reject's attention to the outside world, she felt uncomfortable.

At that, Joan snorted. "Keep that up and I'm going to start thinking we've fallen into a Stephen King novel. It's just a storm, for Pete's sake."

Which was true. But looking again at the two men beside her at the bar, she saw they hadn't lost the tension around their eyes. They didn't like the situation either. It was just a weird storm, though, nothing supernatural or otherwise about it.

Then her gaze trailed back to the window. She saw Reject still sitting there. Erect. Staring out the windows.

"That dog needs some drying off," Josh remarked. "Thing is, he wasn't letting me touch him at all."

"He can find his way to the fire," Joan answered. "That dog never struck me as foolish."

Krystal smiled. "Too true, Mom. None of Harris's sled dogs are foolish, though."

"Too damn smart, if you ask me," Joan retorted.

Almost as if in answer to her, Reject tipped his head back and howled. It was a wolf's howl, long and haunting and strangely beautiful. Everyone in the room froze.

Without a word, Josh rose and walked over to the window, standing beside Reject. The dog howled again. Then he settled down, nose between his front paws, and continued staring out the window.

The room remained quiet, as if everyone knew something important had happened but didn't know what.

Then Josh spoke, causing a stir. "Krystal? Joan? You got some outside lights? Bright ones?"

Krystal didn't hesitate. They had two kinds of outdoor lighting, one soft and warm for deck gatherings, and a brighter set. Security lights, although they'd never been needed that she knew of. She turned those on, figuring they'd be more useful.

In an instant the totally dark afternoon was flooded with light out to the trees beyond and even slightly past them. But somehow the bright lights made the darkness beyond even more secretive. More threatening.

That made no sense to Krystal, who walked over to the windows and stood beside Josh and Reject. "Light made it worse. How is that possible?"

He pointed. "Deeper shadows. Harsher corners. Makes it easier to see if anything approaches, but that's about it."

Krystal nodded, seeing what he referred to. "Some security lights, huh."

He turned to look at her. "They'd scare most people off from approaching. Animals, too. Regardless..."

"Regardless, we should probably turn them off."

He shrugged. "Depends."

"Meaning?" She looked straight at him, and for once his gaze was steady, not at all distant.

"Meaning whether you're more worried about something coming from the dark or seeing something get close to the house."

At that her stomach did a flip. "Damn, Josh!"

He shrugged and resumed looking outside. Just then, Reject lifted his head and let out another long howl. The room behind, which had just started to make friendly noises again, fell completely silent.

"I'd suggest," Josh said quietly, "that lights or no lights you keep these curtains open for a while. Reject sees something."

A shiver ran along Krystal's spine as she heard her worry validated. "I agree. Can you stay long? What about your vets?"

But now she could feel tension in him, as if every nerve and muscle in his body had stretched to the max. "Josh?"

"How much good do you think I'll be here?"

He had a point. Staring out into those strange woods, woods that had never frightened her before, she knew she didn't want him to leave. Something about the way he stood alert made her feel safer.

But she'd also learned something about those vets down there. Vets who couldn't manage the outside world, at least not yet. Was Josh their only link to this reality? What if the storm pushed them over the edge? What might they do?

"You should go," she said presently. Reject howled again, but this time Krystal managed to ignore it. "You've got people to look after."

But Josh didn't move. "Something has that dog stirred up, and I know better than to ignore a dog's senses."

He pulled a small radio from his pocket.

"What's that?"

"Short-range walkie-talkie. Mostly useless in these mountains, but I'll see if I can get Angus."

But he never moved away from the window, even as he managed a crackly conversation.

Josh was staying. That was when Krystal began to seriously wonder what was out there in the storm.

JOSH FELT BETTER after speaking to Angus. Angus had repeatedly proved he could provide a stabilizing force when memories and fears began to get out of hand. He was trusted by their soldiers, as Josh was trusted. But it was still a lot to ask of one man.

But Josh couldn't leave. Not with Reject howling warnings from time to time, as if he sensed something bad approaching. Not when Josh knew that the people in this lodge very likely had no idea how to defend themselves. No, they'd freak with fear.

Like some of his people in the stockade. God, he felt torn in two.

He knew better than to ignore a dog's senses, though. Squatting down, he lowered himself close to the dog's height. Not touching him, not getting in the way of his senses. Reject gave him a long look from those incredible blue husky eyes, sending a message. Josh heeded it.

"Rock and a hard place," he muttered, not wanting to be overheard. But Krystal, who seemed to be glued to his side, heard him. She spoke quietly.

"Are you sure about the dog?"

"I'd trust a dog's sense of danger faster than I'd trust mine, and mine is pretty damn good."

Several minutes, and one more howl from Reject, passed before she spoke again. "What could be out there? A bear?"

Josh didn't disillusion her by arguing that the husky wouldn't be standing guard because of a bear, not when so many humans were around. No, that was the kind of danger most dogs would avoid, not face off. Good survival instincts, especially when a bear wasn't likely to ignore a dog. Not when dogs enraged them.

No, there was something more sinister out there, and from experience Josh could think of only one thing: a human. A human threat.

He spoke quietly. "How many of your lodgers are here right now?"

Krystal turned to look around the room, scanning with the ease of familiarity. "Most of them. Maybe four or five missing."

"Unusual?"

Krystal faced the window again. "Not really. We have some truly introverted people here and we're likely not to see them much at all."

Josh glanced at her. "How the hell do they eat if they don't come in here?"

"Trips to the grocery for supplies. We lay in some for them, occasionally take them hot meals if they're interested."

"Five-star service."

That clearly irritated her a bit. "We provide a place where artists can work undisturbed. That means in every way they want. It's part of the deal, Josh. Do you do any differently for your prisoners?"

At that Josh turned from the window, feeling his face turn as hard as rock, his aquamarine eyes as cold as stone. "Has it ever occurred to any of you judgmental people out here that the stockade is to keep *you* out and not my group in?"

That pierced Krystal visibly, sharply. Even though he'd told her that before, this time he could see that it penetrated the distraction of her own thoughts. This time it reached her like an icy jab in her heart.

"I'm sorry," she said after a moment.

"All you people out here who've never faced the horror my vets have faced should at least do them the courtesy of admitting they have more to fear than their own anger."

Krystal hesitated, then said quietly, "Don't they have drugs for PTSD now?"

"Like they work on everyone. No, sometimes the only thing that can work is knitting the holes in the mind. The places you can't see that the violence tore out of them."

True or not, he hated to make the argument. It sounded as if a cure, or any help, was too far away. Reject howled again and Krystal returned her attention to the window. Someone behind her shouted, "Damn it, can't you shut that dog up?"

It was Josh who turned, speaking in a voice that allowed no disagreement. "Good God, Reject is guarding us. Be glad of it."

Well, that unleashed a cacophony of voices behind Krystal, as people began to argue about the dog, but she obviously didn't want to enter the fray. Guarding them against what? people asked. What should they fear in those woods? They'd never feared them before.

But no one again demanded that Reject shut up.

Joan kept the kitchen staff working constantly. People were eating as much as they were talking, and apparently she felt eating was a better thing.

But Mason's talk the night before last had evidently unleashed something atavistic in these creative people.

Krystal wished sourly that Mason was here for it. Maybe he'd catch a dose of his own medicine.

But as the day wore on, people found it harder and harder to ignore Reject's alert posture. Understandably. The dog wasn't even napping.

Joan and Josh both tried to reach Harris to come check the dog, in case his howling had to do with his injuries. They were still cut off, however, except for Josh's dubious walkie-talkie exchanges with Angus. So far everything seemed okay at the stockade.

But if the lightning hadn't continued to rend the air like a maddened firefight, Josh would have climbed up to the roof to pivot that satellite dish to a position where it could receive and send messages. As it was, every time the thought crossed his mind, lightning flashed again and a gale-force gust of wind ripped through to remind him that nothing could make that dish stay in the right position. Not now. Nor could anyone go up there without risking life and limb.

He wondered how long this storm would last. It seemed like an awfully long time already. He wondered how long Reject would stay alert, refusing even to nap as most dogs did.

He wondered how long his own group, which had grown to nearly twenty men and three women over the past few days, would be able to stand this constant barrage of lightning and thunder before one of them snapped back into the past.

He ought to get his ass down there. But Reject kept him nailed here. The dog had managed to come to the stockade to get someone. But he hadn't remained there. No, he'd made it quite clear that he wanted to be here.

He sighed and looked back at the room, so full of people, and thought about grabbing something to eat. Surely he could stand away from the window for just that long. Reject would signal him.

But just as he had the thought, Reject growled. Deep from somewhere within him emerged the most threatening sound a dog ever made.

Instinctively, Josh tensed. He squatted beside the dog and laid a gentle hand on his shoulder. "What is it, boy?"

Reject spared him the briefest glance from those amazing blue husky eyes, then looked out the window and growled again.

All righty, then. Rising, Josh faced the room. "Get in the back. Get upstairs. Get on the floors. Get away from these windows! *Now!*"

For a moment or two, no one moved, but then the flight began. To Josh's amazement, it was a quiet orderly exodus, most likely aided by the way Joan took over and directed traffic as if this were a drill of some kind. She enlisted her employees from the kitchen as well, and Josh gave them credit for remaining calm through it all.

Krystal joined her mother in directing movement, but only briefly. Soon she was back at the window, beside Josh and Reject.

She spoke quietly. "Maybe we should close the curtains anyway. I feel like a target."

Josh didn't disagree with her, but he had a more important matter to think about: the safety of everyone in this building. He couldn't leave all that to one dog. "Get back behind some furniture. I need to keep an eye out."

She nodded but didn't move. "Okay. The threat will have to shoot all three of us."

Josh felt an instant of amusement. "So sure the threat has a gun?"

"I'm not going all Stephen King here. I refuse to. Mason stirred enough of that up the other night."

"Did he?"

"He's a horror novelist. I guess that's the way he runs. Anyhow, he had plenty of people listening to him. I'm kind of surprised anyone went back to their own cabins that night."

"Then the storm."

"Then the storm," she agreed. "We started filling up."

"I'm not surprised, honestly. This is a pretty violent one."

"More than we're used to around here."

Then his walkie-talkie buzzed. He yanked it off his belt and Angus's voice crackled in answer to his.

"Josh, we're on the move. Protection perimeter and don't ask me to stop it."

Josh swore vigorously as he jammed the walkie back onto his belt.

"Josh? What's that mean?"

He looked at her, and those amazing eyes told a different story this time.

KRYSTAL COULD HARDLY stand his silence. That harsh but sad look that reached the corners of his eyes, that brought them down just a bit. He was worried. Unhappy. Not the pillar of stone she had believed him to be.

Then he turned his head back to the window. "The storm's gotten to my people. Angus can't calm them."

Her stomach quivered uneasily. "So? Now?"

"Angus said perimeter. If that's what they're doing,

it's okay. It's a protection move. The walls are supposed to do that, but I guess they need to feel more in charge."

Krystal gnawed her lower lip, hesitating to press further into all that Josh had clearly placed off-limits with his silences as much as anything. "Josh? What will they do?"

He shook his head. "Guard the compound. Spread out a little. Keep eyes on each other."

She drew a tight breath. "They feel threatened, too."

"That would be my guess."

"So maybe you should go back to them."

Again he looked at her, shaking his head. "These guys know what to do to form a perimeter. No reason they should go beyond that. At least as long as the woods don't start shooting at them or hurling grenades."

The image was ludicrous. It drew a reluctant smile from her, then she saw Josh smile, too. A smile and a brief snort as he shook his head.

"The woods," he said, "aren't the danger."

She stared out into them, misty now with rain. Understanding filled her with skin-crawling unease. "The shadows are."

"Hence Reject."

NEARLY AN HOUR PASSED. Reject didn't growl again. Josh and Krystal eventually pulled some chairs up to the window so they could sit and watch the outdoors. The change brought them some cover, from the waist down. Hardly enough to keep Krystal's skin from crawling, but somewhat better.

Joan at last appeared at the foot of the stairs. "Can we all come down now?"

Just then Reject growled, a sound so low it hardly seemed possible that it came from him.

"Uh, not yet," Krystal answered.

"So a dog is ruling my day," Joan retorted, but she sounded only a tiny bit sarcastic.

"It could be worse," Josh answered.

"As if. I've got nearly fifty people up there who are getting really frustrated. Yeah, Reject's growl scared them. The first few times. But what does it mean?"

"Trouble," Josh answered.

At that instant a bullet zinged and cracked the window not far from Krystal's head.

Reject raised a howl fit to lift the rafters. Josh pushed Krystal to the floor almost before the sound had died away.

"Joan," he said tautly to Krystal's mother.

"Got it," she answered, her voice shaking now. "Close the damn curtains so my daughter isn't a target!"

"I have to be able to see. Krystal can go hide with the rest of you."

"Like hell," Krystal answered, cautiously sitting up. Josh's shove had been forceful enough to leave her shoulder aching. A few pebbles of safety glass rattled on the floor around her.

And Reject, with a dog's amazing instinct, crawled up on her as best he could, sniffing for damage, lingering for sloppy kisses. Krystal hugged him as tightly as she dared given his injured hind leg.

"Guess he wants to take care of you," Josh remarked. "I need to get out there. In this rain, maybe someone left footprints I'll be able to follow."

Fear seized Krystal, gripping her heart. "Josh, no! You could…"

"Get hurt?" he asked almost sarcastically. "Been there, done that. Fear is hardly on my radar any longer. I'm closing these damn curtains, you pay attention to Reject's warnings, and I'm going to get my butt out there to find the gunman. The silly part just went out of this entire experience."

Krystal couldn't argue with that. A gunshot. Through a window. Maybe intended for her. Maybe intended for Josh. The two of them hadn't been that far apart, after all.

But hadn't they been acting kind of silly for hours now? Wedded to this window and a dog? But she had to admit that the bullet had changed everything. Reject's behavior had given her the creeps, but now it went far beyond some spooky horror novel feeling. This was real.

Josh drew the curtains quickly enough with the electronic controls. At least the generator out back had started running an hour or so ago, but other things could go wrong. Plenty of them.

Insulated curtains approached a near blackout. Other windows had the same protection against the ice of winter. Now protection against something even more life-threatening.

God. She watched Josh pull on his poncho, watched Reject whine a bit as Josh left, then wondered what to do with the curtains closed.

Her mother soon answered that question, coming down the stairs. "I guess we can come down now. Nobody can see in here. Where's Josh?"

"Out hunting a gunman."

Joan just shook her head. "Put men in a uniform and they all think they're invincible."

Krystal didn't think that was fair, but she wasn't about to argue the matter. She watched Reject closely, afraid she might miss a warning, afraid she might see one.

A quieter crowd, minus a few who preferred to stay upstairs, gathered in the great room. Some even had an appetite, amazingly enough. Krystal didn't think she could have swallowed a thing even if she hadn't eaten in a week.

Reluctant to leave the window because of the dog, who still stared toward the curtained expanse, Krystal realized she trusted Reject's senses. She couldn't see anything out there herself. Glancing around the room, she caught sight of Mary Collins sitting alone at a table and went over to join her. Mary had been a late arrival in the lodge today. One of their true introverts, almost always alone by choice.

"How are you doing?" she asked Mary as she slid into a seat facing her. "This hasn't been a fun day so far."

Mary smiled faintly. As usual, the expression was a bit sour and unattractively framed by her oily, thin hair. "The dog has been fun."

"Quite a trip, isn't he?" Krystal was growing fonder of Reject by the minute. "I'm hoping Harris will let me keep him." Although Harris had already made it clear that Reject decided for himself. Maybe it wasn't Harris she was worried about when it came to Reject.

Mary looked over at the curtained window where Reject appeared to still be standing guard.

"He's bright enough. But what do you suppose is bothering him out there?"

Krystal shook her head. "Something. A bullet went

through that window. You heard, I'm sure." A hollow sound, echoing in this huge room.

Mary shuddered. "I did. I almost forgot that."

How anyone could forget that bullet surpassed Krystal's understanding, but then, Mary often appeared lost in her own world. Truly involved in whatever she was writing.

Krystal leaned her chin on her hand, trying not to think about Josh out there. Trying not to worry about him. "Got any advice for writer's block?"

At that, Mary's face brightened. "Stop trying to write your book."

Krystal frowned faintly. "And how's that supposed to help?"

Mary shrugged. "It'll take the pressure off. Just spend fifteen minutes in the morning writing about anything that crosses your mind, then walk away."

Krystal sighed. "Seems strange."

"Sure it does. But somehow it takes away the fear and the words start flowing."

"Is that what you do?"

Mary's tone grew wry. "More than I'd like to admit."

"Then I'll try it." Anything sounded better than staring at a blank computer screen. "This doesn't seem like a good time, though."

Mary surprised her with a grin. "Well, you could try one of Mason's horror stories."

Krystal couldn't help it. She looked toward the covered windows and the dog.

Mary asked, "Where's that guy from the stockade?"

"Out looking for a gunman."

"God!" Mary shuddered. "He must be nuts."

"Or a trained soldier."

Silence followed. Then Mary tilted her head. "I hadn't thought of that."

Who had around here, Krystal wondered. Mostly a vague sense of curiosity washed away by their own preoccupations. Not since last year when the stockade had made its final appearance with those log walls had anyone paid any real attention. And that had faded away as some decided the structure simply added to the local charm. People in this retreat weren't especially interested in what was happening outside.

But that was the entire point of this place, wasn't it?

Except that she hated the idea that Josh was out there conducting a lone search. And what the hell had he meant about his group forming a perimeter? A perimeter around what? Against what?

Again that uneasy sensation of something supernatural washed through her. She had to struggle to make it go away. She simply didn't believe that stuff, was willing to suspend her disbelief occasionally for a good novel—the exception being Mason's—but only for that. Things didn't go bump in her night.

But another look at Reject dissolved all her resolutions. The fur along his spine and neck had risen. A silent warning.

Why silent now? God, where was Josh? Should she send everyone upstairs? Had the threat grown closer?

The storm decided to join the act, stepping up the wind until the rain rattled under the porch roof against the windows, sounding almost like a hail of bullets.

Suddenly all Krystal could think of was the way they

were cut off from the world, not even a satellite phone. No way to summon help.

Then Reject turned away from the window and faced the front door.

God, what now? Krystal wished for a weapon, any weapon, but she doubted a steak knife would provide much protection. Maybe a chef's knife out of the kitchen.

Then, from out of her distant childhood, she remembered the pilot's voice coming over the loudspeakers on a flight she had taken a few weeks after 9/11. "Just remember there's more of us than them."

Before she could find her voice to repeat that, the front door banged open and Josh entered, a woman in his arms. The agent, Darlene Dana, lay almost unconscious, dressed in jeans and a flannel shirt, her usual costume when she visited Mason. No *Vogue* about her now.

"Get her warm," he ordered, his voice sharp.

"What happened?" demanded a few people.

"She was running through the rain. Mason Cambridge is dead."

THE SHOCK PASSED QUICKLY, possibly because news of Mason Cambridge's demise didn't feel like a major loss to many of them. Regardless, several women moved forward. Josh laid Dana on the sofa near a fireplace and the women quickly stripped her and wrapped her in the afghans that had lain cheerily across the back of every padded piece of furniture in the room.

After a few minutes, Darlene Dana's eyes fluttered open and she groaned.

"It's going to hurt for a few minutes," Josh said, his tone

as reassuring as any Krystal had ever heard anywhere. "You got pretty hypothermic."

Joan arrived almost instantly. "Broth okay?" she asked Josh.

"Slowly."

Joan leaned down with a mug in her hand. "It's not too hot, I checked. Let me know when you want a sip, okay?"

Such a small thing, but so important, Krystal thought. Then she looked around and realized the whole damn room was beginning to cluster around Darlene Dana. Wouldn't that make her feel good, to be peppered with questions when she had just run in terror through the most god-awful storm?

She looked around. "Hey, people, back up and give Darlene some room. Give her a chance to recover." At once, however reluctantly, the group backed up and began to sit at tables.

Josh had retreated a short distance to a chair beside a dining table. "Not much she can tell you that I can't, anyway. I reached Cambridge's cabin first. He'd been shot. Then I found Darlene tearing through the woods, sobbing her eyes out, terrified of me. Had to calm her like a scared horse."

Gazes tracked back to Darlene, then once again to Josh.

"Murder?" someone breathed, drawing gasps from everyone.

"Maybe," Josh answered. "I gather this guy wasn't a favorite here. Regardless, I'm no expert. We need the sheriff."

"And we can't call him," Davis said. "Hell's bells."

Bodies shifted. Apparently no one felt it necessary to

cluster yet, but their gazes all turned to Reject, who oddly had finally seemed to relax.

"I'll try the landline again," Joan said. "No reason it should be down from this damn storm. I just don't get it."

But something had cut off all communication with the outside world including the landline. Josh gave a slight shake of his head and pulled the walkie off his belt. The sound crackled worse than before. "Angus? You still got a perimeter?"

The answering crackle sounded affirmative.

"Then get 'em up here. This retreat needs more guarding. We found a body."

When he disconnected he looked around at a room of stunned faces. "We still need a sheriff. And y'all are going to have to get used to my vets being out there. They'll make you as safe as possible."

JOSH KNEW HE was looking at a bunch of unpredictable people. There was no certainty about how any of them might act, and how the hysteria of one might transmit to the others. He could keep his people outside pretty much in line, but the ones in here?

Not a person in this crowd was accustomed to discipline, to taking orders. To following directions unquestioningly. Any one of them might go off the deep end.

He drew Krystal aside, giving her the best warning he could. "Watch 'em, Krys. Somebody might get some crazy idea."

"Yeah, like a book I keep trying to forget." She shook her head as if she could shake something out of it. "These are imaginative people, Josh. No telling which way that imagination will run."

"My concern exactly. Besides, the human mind is built that way. I've seen it in a desolate outpost in Afghanistan. Enough darkness, enough isolation, a few weird sounds. Doesn't take much."

Krystal scanned the room again. "How can I keep an eye on so many people?"

"Watch them cluster. Clustering should give you a feel for how people are thinking. Anyway, it must be time to feed them again. That always helps calm people. Ask for your mother's help."

TALK ABOUT SURREAL. Krystal helped prepare a simple meal of soup, roasts, veggies and the last of the bread that had come from Melinda's bakery in town only yesterday. An ordinary meal.

Yet so unordinary. Curtains closed tight against the darkness. They almost never did that because the clients liked the soft glow of the porch lights through the windows. A number always liked to eat at the wooden tables outside on the deck when the evening was pleasant enough.

No one was outside. No one even glanced at the curtains. Krystal could almost feel the awareness of everyone in the room of the hole in the window. A single bullet that might have been directed or might simply have been intended to scare. They avoided looking at the area that had caused them alarm.

Krystal bit her lip so hard she feared cutting it. Avoiding the situation wasn't going to help any of them deal with the reality that they were locked in this building with a killer out there. Or in here with them? God, she couldn't bear the thought, running like ice through every vein in her body. In *here*? It couldn't be. Someone had shot out the window from the outside, not the inside. No, the killer was out there in the dark storm somewhere.

Mason Cambridge dead. Krystal had always thought rather ungenerously that his ego would keep him going another hundred years. Gone. It felt impossible.

His agent, shivering less now, still had eyes so frightened they were terrifying to look into. No one glanced Darlene Dana's way now, as if she had become a symbol of the day's peculiar terror. Surreal.

Surreal that they showed more attention to a dog who lay alert in front of the curtained windows, though he had long since grown silent.

Nothing about the evening felt real. It was almost like slipping into that Dalí painting of the melting watches. Nothing looked quite right. As if everything were distorted.

Krystal tried to shake her mood as she filled the buffet and stacked clean dishes at the ends of it. Tonight there would be no individual service. Too few employees had been able to get to the lodge because of the storm.

Wine and liquor were the first items claimed from the cash bar. Hardly surprising. More slowly, plates of food were filled and people carried their own napkin-wrapped utensils to the table. Evidently not all the factors of real life had vanished in this haven.

But this haven wasn't feeling like one at all. She watched Josh at a distance, talking on his walkie-talkie. It would have been nice to know what was being said.

But finally he approached her. "One of my guys is taking the extra Humvee down the hill to town to get the sheriff."

"Thank God!"

"It's going to be a rough ride. It looks like some of the road may be washing out."

Krystal closed her eyes. Surreal. More and more surreal. This never happened. "Anything else?" she asked finally, dreading the answer.

"You said some people still hadn't shown up here. Are they still missing?"

Chapter Six

Krystal's heart stopped. Fear raced through her. A murdered man out there and missing people? She scanned the room quickly, trying to make no mistakes. "Oh, God," she murmured. "Four of our greatest introverts. It's not unusual for them to fail to show up here."

She dragged her gaze to his. He was already looking tougher, as if it came as second nature. His voice became hard as steel.

"I guess I'd better look, at least to make sure they're safe in their cabins."

She nodded. "I'll go with you. These people know me and won't be frightened by seeing a stranger. I'll get Joan to take charge here."

Josh scanned the room. "It won't take us long, will it? Just so she doesn't have to handle much by herself."

Krystal shook her head. "We aim for privacy, not distance." Then she smiled slightly. "My mother is tougher than she looks. Trust me."

Joan was frankly unhappy about her daughter going out into this storm with a killer out there somewhere, but she'd learned a long time ago that getting into an argument with Krystal seldom served any use. She spread the map of the cabins, as if Krystal didn't know where they all were, tutting the entire time, but making sure Josh got a good look.

"Just don't take too long," she said sharply. "God, you're going to give me a heart attack."

"You've been saying that for years and you're still here," Krystal teased her. She received only the faintest, tightest of smiles from Joan. Well, that hadn't worked.

Then she and Josh pulled on ponchos, his a camo and hers a bright yellow, and together they prepared to step into a wet, blustery day that seemed more full of rage than a regular thunderstorm. Reject wanted to come along but Krystal eased him back. "Don't want you getting your leg wet out here." He remained, looking droopy.

She tightened the drawstring around her hood and left the snaps down the sides closed. For some reason she ordinarily preferred not to be so enclosed in the garment, but this day offered no alternative.

Then the two of them set out along the stone-edged path. "Paul Aston is out this way," she remarked. "A poet. He *really* doesn't like to be disturbed."

"Let's hope he hasn't been disturbed at all."

Krystal shared his hope. Mason was enough. One death. This wasn't a mystery novel, and she didn't want corpses strewn around the retreat. Although she didn't want to think about it, she was truly distressed by Mason's death. Easier to keep it from the forefront of her mind. As if it would recede.

Paul's cabin was about one hundred and fifty feet back from the main trail. Lights glowed from lanterns and he answered the knock on his door immediately, dressed in rumpled denim with his wisps of gray hair springing every which way.

"What do you want?" he groused. "My computer and power aren't working. Of course, working on poetry by lamplight and with handwriting isn't the worst creative situation." Those benefits didn't keep him from scowling at Krystal, however.

Krystal spoke soothingly. "We just wanted to make sure you're okay."

"As okay as I can be without modern conveniences. I paid for them, you know." Then he slammed the door.

"So much for telling him to be careful," Josh remarked. "Nice guy."

"We don't get paid to entertain only nice people and they don't pay to have us provide less than perfection." A situation that sometimes aggravated her half to death.

Josh snorted. "When you meet perfection, let me know."

They took a turn to the right, heading for the next cabin.

"Don't you have a hand map of this place?" Josh asked.

"The only one is the one you saw in my mother's office. Otherwise we'll rely on my memory."

"A map would sure be useful when my group gets out here."

She turned her head to eye him. His face was only partly visible in the gloom. Then a flash of nearby lightning nearly blinded her. "God!" she said loudly.

"If that was a heavenly comment, I'm sure I don't want to be on the receiving end."

Krystal heard the humor in his voice and felt relieved. If she had to be out here hunting for guests in this awful storm, she couldn't think of a better companion. "So this perimeter thing you mentioned?"

"My people will fan out around this retreat, keeping

an eye out for intruders. Like sentries. That's why a map would be useful."

"I can see that. But why should they help?"

"Because it's who they are," he answered levelly. "Still. Despite everything."

Krystal had a strong feeling that she shouldn't ask about the *everything*. This group had been present across the creek from her for a year now and little knowledge of them escaped. Very little. Privacy seemed to be as important across the creek as it was here.

"So where's the name come from," Josh asked. "Cash Creek Canyon?"

"A century and a half ago. Interesting bit of history. A couple of places in these mountains were discovered to have gold. Not so much here, but placer mining continued for a couple of decades."

"Placer?" he asked.

"Rinsing gold from the water. Anyway, that's the Cash Creek part."

"And the creek itself was part of finding gold? And the canyon, too?"

"The placer mining, yes. But there was another advantage to the creek and canyon. It joins up with several other creeks and small rivers that run down the slopes from snowmelt and springs. You might have seen the reservoir up there?"

"Yeah. Kinda big."

"Kinda necessary. For a long time the creeks and rivers joined together to make the larger river that Conard City was built around. Eventually it wasn't reliable enough water and it needed to reach a lot more land, like ranches, so the reservoir was built."

"You're right. It's interesting history," he remarked presently as the lights of another cabin began to show. "Who is this?"

"Giselle Bibe, commonly called Gizzie. PhD student. She's taking a sabbatical here to write her dissertation."

"Tough job, I hear. Better written indoors than out, though." Meant as a touch of humor, she could tell.

Krystal didn't much feel like smiling when the wind chose that moment to blow icy raindrops into her face. Drops that felt almost like sleet, although given the altitude and despite the time of year sleet was entirely possible. As was snow, God forbid.

Gizzie seemed to be doing a whole lot better than Paul Aston. Her half frame readers were perched on the end of her nose and she greeted them with a smile. "You ought to come in for some coffee. And what the dickens are you doing out, anyway? I wouldn't call it hospitable."

Josh let Krystal answer. "Given the severity of the storm and the lack of power, we just wanted to check on people who didn't come to the dining room."

"Well, I'm doing just fine," Gizzie assured them. "Rather nice to be writing in a situation that echoes the history around here. A whole lot more atmospheric, too, without power. No problems, so don't worry about me."

Krystal decided to take it one step further. Hardly knowing what reaction to expect, she clenched her hands tightly. "Mason Cambridge is dead. You might not want to be out here alone."

"Hah! So he finally bought it? I wondered how a man so choleric could fail to have a fatal heart condition. Well, don't worry about me. I can keep company with his damn ghost, no problem."

As they walked away, Josh spoke. "Maybe we need to be stronger in the warning."

"But we don't know if some killer is after anyone else. Besides, Mason would have been a target for darn near everyone here. The *only* target."

A snort of laughter escaped Josh. "I *do* like you, Krystal Metcalfe."

"I'm being nasty."

"So go for it. Wanna have a competition?"

But she'd heard his suggestion that they make a stronger warning. She decided to be firmer with the others and pick up Gizzie on the way back.

Then he pulled the walkie out from under his poncho and tried again. This time the signal was a little clearer.

"Rusty figures he's halfway down to the town," Angus answered Josh. "As for the rest of us, the perimeter is spreading. Maybe you should let people know we'll be out there. No heart attacks on my watch, please."

"Not likely," Josh answered. "Anyway, there are no comms out here to tell folks about you guys. I mentioned it earlier, anyway. But nobody's going to see you, right?"

"Better not or we'll have a course on using rusty skills around here."

When Josh disconnected, Krystal said, "I like the sound of that man."

"Utterly reliable. Good-hearted, too."

As Krystal had begun to suspect, Josh was as well. After all, he'd been the one to take Reject for help. Some people wouldn't have gone to so much trouble for a dog.

But then, some people didn't value the lives of animals.

"How many more do we need to check up on?" Josh asked.

"Two more, I think. Julia and Sebastian are probably okay, though. A long way from Mason's cabin." Then she bit her lower lip. "I don't suppose I need to go inside the cabins if no one answers?"

He paused midstride and looked at her. She stared at him, once again noting how attractive he was even when he looked like rugged stone.

"Krystal," he said quietly, "I'm going to give you a couple of reasons you don't want to go in any of these cabins. The first is you don't want to mess up a possible crime scene for the cops. I imagine Darlene Dana probably did enough of that at Mason's place."

She nodded. "You're right. I didn't think of that."

"I figured. Then there's the second reason. Take me at my word. Whatever might have happened in another cabin you don't want the images haunting you for the rest of your life."

She stood frozen as unwanted pictures flooded her mind anyway. She was sure her ideas couldn't be as bad as reality. What did she know about it, anyway? Scenes from movies?

Josh reached out and took her forearm gently. "Bad enough what might have happened in there. Absolutely no need for you to see anything. Now let's go make sure the rest of these loners are okay."

And Krystal, very suddenly, didn't want to think about that at all. She'd been assuming only one person had been hurt, and that was a huge assumption under the circumstances.

"Damn, Josh," she muttered quietly.

"Take it easy," he said kindly. "If anyone doesn't open their door, I'll go in. Not you. Absolutely not you. And there's no reason to think that anyone else has been hurt, right?"

Small comfort considering what Josh might find. That they'd have another reason to wait for a deputy. For law enforcement and crime scene teams…

Given the way Darlene had reacted to her discovery of Mason's body, expecting a horrific sight was not beyond belief. She was hardly aware of crossing her fingers inside her gloves.

Julia Jansen, a watercolorist, proved to be all right and more than eager to join the group at the lodge. She didn't even argue when Josh insisted she don her rain gear and come with him and Krystal while they checked on the last absent resident. This storm was clearly upsetting her.

It was certainly one of the most violent Krystal could remember having seen in these mountains. The wind threatened to knock them over as they pushed their way to the last cabin.

Where they found another writer dead. Josh didn't let anyone enter, but Julia began to keen helplessly when she heard that Sebastian Elsin was dead.

"Everybody back to the lodge now," Josh ordered, his voice like steel. "Now!"

Neither Julia nor Krystal hesitated to hurry down the path, their flashlights their only guide. Behind her, she heard Josh get on his walkie again.

"Update" was all he said. A few seconds later, he added one word. "Good."

Then he drew closer to the women. "We're sweeping up that Aston guy and that woman on our way back. Nobody's going to be out here alone. Got it?"

Krystal gave him a firm yes. Julia sounded fainter. Josh spoke again. "The perimeter is tightening. Eyes are on us. We should get back to the lodge safely."

Chapter Seven

The lodge was unwontedly still, except for the storm that raged outside as if it wanted to wipe the planet clear.

Josh moved to the back room that was Joan's office and Krystal followed, not caring if he wanted her there or not. He was planning and she needed to be part of it. She needed to be able to do something except pace. Except want to scream at the horror of all this. She kept a lid on her self-control, but it wasn't easy.

And Josh was still stuck on the walkie-talkie. It didn't seem possible that communications had been out this long. The handyman, Mel, could usually resight the satellite dish on the rare occasions it got out of alignment. But not in this storm.

People were too quiet, Krystal thought. Joan, in an attempt at cheer, moved through the lodge with her limited staff, serving up menus and drinks. Not much food was being ordered—not that the kitchen could provide much with a short staff.

"All right, I got it," Josh said finally. He had Joan's unrolled map of the retreat spread on the table and was freely marking it up. What the X's meant, Krystal had no idea.

But at last he seemed done with talking in a foreign

language, or at least it sounded like it, what with the military jargon he was probably using.

"So, what's going on?" Krystal asked, unwilling to be kept in the dark. At times like these, Josh didn't look like a man anyone should disagree with. A slight shiver ran down her spine. Dangerous. He could be dangerous.

He shook his head. "There aren't enough people in my group to provide a tight cordon. Which isn't to say they won't be working double-time, but they'll probably have to pull in closer, which could make them more visible. I don't like that."

She nodded, understanding that he had to be concerned about a threat to his soldiers. But also about how people in the lodge might react if they happened to see them in numbers. "We'll just remind everyone…"

"Remind everyone of what? That they'll actually *see* a bunch of former soldiers surrounding them? Where's *that* trust supposed to come from?"

Krystal wanted to curse, hating the fact that he was probably right. Over the years she'd heard the casual talk from people who had no comparable experience. People who didn't grasp the price of war. People who distrusted vets because they "might go ballistic" at any moment.

She also didn't miss the bitterness in Josh's tone. "Maybe you ought to make a point of becoming neighbors around here." Even as she spoke she wished she could snatch the ugly words back. As near as she could tell, Josh's group didn't feel like they had neighbors, good or bad.

"Damn it, Krys, how many times do I have to tell you that stockade is protection for my people from the outside world. The world they still can't tolerate. A reality they might never quite join again. A reality that just keeps on wounding them."

She felt an ache deep within her. "I'm sorry. I guess I'm just not getting it."

He tossed a pencil onto the map. "Why should you? It's an alien experience."

Then his walkie crackled and the now familiar voice of Angus came through. "Sheriff's on his way up. He's got a few Humvees so it shouldn't take too long. Body count still at two?"

"Yeah. We think we have everyone rounded up safely. At least for the retreat area. God knows what might be happening in the town." He disconnected.

Krystal's heart had plummeted to her toes. She hadn't even thought of the town, although the oversight was probably the result of the first murder having been Mason. At this point the artists seemed like the obvious targets.

Josh astonished her by reaching out and gently snaking an arm around her. "You look as lost as just about anybody I've known. We'll work the problem. We'll solve it. And reinforcements are arriving, courtesy of the Conard County Sheriff's Department."

Then he gave her a gentle squeeze and released her.

But that hug, brief as it had been, had relaxed a deep tension inside her. Her confidence grew, and she suspected that Josh deserved every bit of her trust.

They left her mother's office, the map remaining behind. Josh made the announcement to the great room, which was still subdued. "The sheriff's deputies are on the way up here. They'll add to your protection and try to find out what's going on. For now, I'd say everyone in this room is safe from an outside threat."

He didn't directly mention his people out there, watching from all sides.

Josh and Krystal sat at a table. Joan brought them glasses of red wine and menus. "Eat," she ordered. "Both of you look like something the cat dragged in."

For the first time since early that morning, Krystal felt truly hungry, as if her mother had given her a subliminal suggestion.

Josh ordered hugely from the menu, offering no apologies for the size of his appetite. Krystal decided to follow suit. Who was going to tell her two hamburgers and fries was too much? Not even herself, not today.

Slowly the room around them began to hum with voices, and meals started to be gathered from the buffet. It was as if Josh had calmed everyone, maybe with the promise the sheriff was on the way.

Halfway through her too-large meal, Krystal spoke to Josh. "I can see one murder. But why would there be two?"

Josh shrugged a shoulder. "That's for the cops to figure out." Then he half smiled. "We can speculate, though."

She had to smile back at him. "Speculation can be fun."

"Sure can. Unless we turn it into some kind of horror conspiracy."

Her smile fled. "That's sort of what Mason was doing the other night. You should have seen our crowd. He had them going almost as much as word of his murder did."

"Not the kind of person you need to have around right now."

"I figured he was rehearsing his next book. It would have been spooky enough."

Seemingly out of nowhere, Joan plopped herself at their table. She kept her voice low, even though the conversation in the room was growing louder, as if from the approach of the sheriff. As if from the approach of the sense of security the news gave them.

"How about you tell me," Joan said to Josh, "just why you were marking up my map? Looked like a ring to me, and I have a right to know what you're doing on my land."

Josh clearly hesitated. His gaze grew distant, as if he saw something miles away, then snapped back to look at Joan.

"My group is out there creating a perimeter of protection. In theory, anything crosses their barrier and we'll know it."

Joan nodded slowly. "And you're not giving us details of them surrounding us because…?"

Krystal spoke. "Because there's an army out there ringed around us. You want to create a panic, Mom?"

Joan drew a deep breath, looking nearly shocked. "Sad to say…" She shook her head. "Okay. I'll feed your people when they can come in."

Josh answered, his voice hard again, "You'll never see most of them. And that's the way they want it."

Even as the room began to recover its life, even as the storm seemed to quiet down a bit outside, a dome of silence seemed to settle over the table where the three of them sat.

"You know," Joan remarked eventually, "I've lived my entire life right here and I can't recall a storm this bad. But then, I can't recall two murders either."

IT FELT LIKE forever to Krystal, but at last flashing blue and red lights appeared, splintered through the stained glass of the double front doors.

Nobody moved. Except Josh. "Stop the stampede if you can," he said to Joan and Krystal, then strode quickly to the doors.

He wasn't far from his description of a stampede. Everyone wanted to get outside to the safety of the sheriff's presence.

Josh paused at the door and spoke loudly, demanding attention. "Stay where you are. We don't know what's out there. We don't want to interfere with the law." He saw Krystal and Joan moving swiftly through the knots of their clients, speaking quietly. Soothingly. The urgent rush to the door eased.

Then he stepped outside into the bath of swirling lights from roof racks and bumpers on three Humvees.

A tall man covered in a yellow slicker, with his cowboy hat protected by an elastic version, stepped out of the first vehicle. He held out a hand to Josh.

"I'm Dalton," he said. "If you recall from the sled dog place. And you're Josh from the compound, as I remember."

Josh nodded. So the sheriff had checked him out beyond the light interview last year from a deputy and since their meeting at Harris's place. Probably knew everything there was to know about the guys at the stockade, too. Well, that would make things easier.

"Two murders?" Dalton asked. As he turned his head, Josh caught sight again of the shiny burn scar that covered most of Dalton's face. The man had clearly known his share of hell. Josh's confidence in the help they'd receive rose a few notches.

"How are you sure they're murders?" Dalton asked.

"Seen enough of it. First one was a bullet to the head. Execution-style from the back."

"So the perp probably knew the attacker."

"Maybe." The thought of Mason's agent danced across his mind. But while the author might be difficult to deal with, why would Darlene Dana cut off her cash cow?

"And the other?"

"A whole lot messier. Stab wounds. One shot that misdirected to a femoral artery."

"Hmm." Dalton rubbed his chin. "Same perp? Different methods. Maybe not so easy the second time. Or maybe the killer was having trouble stomaching the first killing."

Josh shook his head. "Knife wounds hardly indicate sudden squeamishness. But it could have been the other way around, stabbing first. You guys will know better than I can."

"Reckon so." Then Gage faced him directly. "You got your guys out here, that man of yours said when he came down the mountain. Perimeter?"

Josh nodded. "I'll call 'em back if you want. Hell, they'd probably like to get to the stockade themselves. Right now, between us, we've got a lot of folks out there, maybe starting to step on each other with your people."

Gage turned a little to the right, staring into the rain and still-rumbling storm. "If you can keep 'em out there, to help my deputies, I'd be grateful. Up to them, of course. I need to send a few people inside to start questioning the residents here, but I don't exactly have a crowd of deputies with me. Storm's causing trouble down the mountain, too."

Josh hesitated. "My soldiers don't want much interaction, Sheriff. Makes 'em uncomfortable. Sometimes too uncomfortable to endure."

"I get it. I'll tell my units to tread carefully. We just need eyes on this situation. The more the better. Yours would be helpful."

Josh understood from a tactical point of view. But he also knew that coming out to help with this operation had already been a sore trial for his vets. "I can only ask them. I stopped giving orders years ago."

"Fair enough." Then with a hand signal, Dalton began to unload his Humvees. Several deputies he sent inside. The rest he began to arrange in accord with his own terrain map spread under a light in the front seat of one of the vehicles. He asked Josh to point out the two cabins where the murders had happened and where he thought his own troops might be.

Then the criminal part of the investigation began.

COMMS STILL HADN'T come back and Josh was reaching a level of frustration unusual for him. Damn it, he needed to be able to coordinate his unit easily. The sheriff needed that.

And yeah, war had put him in such situations before, but that didn't mean he liked it. Everything became ten times as difficult.

Inside he found two deputies, a man and a woman, dominating the setup, sitting at a table. A couple of other deputies wandered around casually, as if hoping to overhear something that wouldn't emerge in direct questioning. They'd all shed their yellow rain gear, revealing the comforting sight of their police uniforms.

And they *were* bringing comfort. Josh felt as if the air inside the room had changed. As if the pressure had vanished.

This crew of artists might still make it through this situation without developing crazy ideas and opposing plans of operation. No growth of opposing camps that he could see. Plenty of reason to be grateful for that.

Joan handed out insulated carafes of coffee to the deputies along with sweet rolls. Both were received with gratitude.

But the questioning began, as it had to. The smallest piece of information might be important.

And they started with the most terrified witness of all: Darlene Dana. That woman still trembled, as if she couldn't grasp what she had seen that morning. As if it were beyond her to accept the harsh reality.

Some matters could definitely be harder to accept than others. The sad thing was when you started to accept them as a normal part of reality. Soldiers knew that. That's why he had a stockade full of them.

Back in Joan's office, he began to get in touch with his group as best he could. Hardly surprising to him was the way these guys wanted to stay on duty. They were doing something useful, following plans that had once been part of their lives. Becoming themselves again.

Nine steps back in their recovery but Josh wouldn't have deprived them of renewed feelings of usefulness. Not for any reason. They needed it. They could and would catch up later with their work toward recovery. These soldiers were filled with determination and grit.

He joined Krystal at a table out front.

"Hard to believe," she said, "that this has been going on for almost a day."

"Getting late," he agreed, glancing at his watch.

"Nobody is going to sleep for a while."

He smiled faintly. "Does that surprise you?"

"No." She laughed quietly. "It'll be interesting to watch them crash out eventually."

Then she looked around at the room in a way that troubled him. He could almost see her shudder, then she spoke. "I can't believe that one of the people here is a murderer."

"Always the quiet ones." Josh cited a canard he'd never quite believed. He sipped the coffee Joan had swung by to deliver.

"So they claim. But this place is full of quiet types. That one isn't going to work here."

"Maybe not. But why don't you tell me about the people you've gotten to know, at least a little."

She clearly gave that some thought. "Like I might pick up a clue?"

"Why not? That deputy over there, what's her name? Connie Parish? She's going to be asking you for the same information before long."

"Probably. Except you wouldn't let me see much out there at the cabins, so what do I know?"

"Just as well. Trust me. So tell me about the people around us. That's what you *do* know."

Krystal returned her attention to the groups of residents. "Well, there's Paul Aston, over there with the sloppy clothes and almost no hair. You gathered him up earlier."

"Still manages an Einstein look."

Krystal nodded. "You ever figure out how he does that with so little hair, let me know."

"So, what about him?"

"Poet, which doesn't mean anything by itself. Just that he's more introverted than most. In any summer we'll hardly see him, unless he feels a need to walk in the woods. Even then it's a rare sighting."

"I hear poets don't make a lot of money."

Her mouth lifted at one corner. "You hear right."

"So how's he manage to come here?"

"Scholarship. We do a few every year."

Josh nodded, absorbing the information. "What makes him special?"

"He's got a name, if not money. Once in a while he'll even talk to some of our clients who are interested in poetry. Not very often, though."

"So, like a box-office draw?"

Finally he pulled a laugh from her. Quiet, but still a genuine laugh. "Yeah. Good name to have on the annual flyer."

He twisted on his chair, leaning toward her. "What about this Mason guy?"

Krystal leaned back, sighing. "God, that man is—was— a piece of work. I don't think I've ever met anyone with a bigger ego and he didn't care who knew it. Abrasive. I'll never understand why he always had a coterie of followers when he showed up here for meals. It was like he was holding court and loved every minute of it. I honestly don't know how his agent could stand him."

"Money," Josh said flatly. "Bestseller?"

"Always. And if you want my opinion," she burst out, "I never saw a man more likely to become a murder victim."

"Whoa," Josh said quietly.

Krystal looked away, plainly embarrassed by her outburst.

Josh reached across the table and squeezed her hand gently. "I wasn't telling you to stop. Not criticizing you.

Just kind of amazed that the guy created such an impression."

"He wasn't forgettable. Ever."

Connie Parish took that moment to come to their table with a notepad. She sat, looking at the two of them. "You were at the beginning of all this?"

"Depends on where you want to begin," Krystal answered. "Someone shot one of Harris Belcher's sled dogs and left it outside Josh's stockade. At least they were able to rescue the animal and Harris was able to take care of it. Then Reject adopted me." She pointed with her chin toward the dog, who was sleeping on a braided rug by the windows.

Connie's brows lifted. "Well, that's definitely a point of interest. Nobody should want to shoot one of Harris's dogs."

"According to Harris, they'd have had to remove him from his kennel. Then they took him a ways into the forest before they shot him."

Connie swore. "Some things I will never understand. Others I know too well." She looked at Josh. "I'm sure you do, too. So you folks saved the dog?"

Josh nodded.

Krystal shook her head. "I can't remember everything in order, Connie. It's been too much today. Josh came over to tell us about the dog. He was pretty angry with all of us, but he also felt it was some kind of message to his group."

That caught Connie's full attention. "Reason for that?"

Josh's mouth twisted. "Give me one reason anyone around here would be happy with our group holed up in that stockade like hermits. Thought maybe someone wanted us to leave."

Connie nodded. "You guys don't strike me as the leaving type."

"We aren't."

Krystal again saw that steel in Josh. The man who could probably handle just about anything. No, he had no intention of leaving or of taking away the protection he was giving his own people.

"Okay," Connie said after she'd made a note. "How did things unfold with Mason's murder? I'm starting to get the impression that no one in this room is particularly surprised by it or very upset by it. Except his agent."

Krystal answered frankly, "You'd probably be right. Not well-liked except by a few. If any."

Connie made another note, then turned to Josh again. "You guys keep to yourselves, if I understand correctly. What were you doing over here when the murder happened?"

That almost sounded like an accusation. Krystal stiffened but Josh remained relaxed.

"I came to bring Reject, the injured dog, to Krystal. He apparently preferred to be with her over me. Understandable." Josh sounded ever so slightly sarcastic. "Anyway, when we got back here, Reject started getting upset at the windows. First howling like he was on watch. Then growling, so I went out to find out what was bugging him enough to growl. That's when I found Darlene Dana a soaked mess at the edge of the woods."

"A *terrified* mess," Krystal added. "I don't think I've ever seen anyone so scared."

More notes for Connie. "So the dog alerted?"

Josh answered, "He acted like there was something out there that he didn't like at all. The growl was such a change, such a deep one, that I became convinced that whatever was out there was seriously bad."

"And your guys started a perimeter."

Josh looked stony, as if he expected criticism. "Yeah. They started closing in around this place."

"Anyway," Krystal said, picking up the story because she understood how Josh must feel, given the protectiveness he'd shown toward his group. She didn't want him to feel attacked once again. "Josh asked me if anyone was missing from our gathering here. Then we went out looking for them. And that's when we found Sebastian Elsin dead, too. Uglier, from what Josh said."

"So it's been a long day for you guys."

Krystal glanced at the clock over one of the fireplaces. Nearly 3:00 a.m. "Slightly."

"And Gage has been out this way twice. Once for the dog report. Then after all the communications failed and you all had your guy come down to town to report murder."

There didn't seem to be any response needed. It was the way things had unfolded. A few days that had grown darker and uglier from the point when Reject had been injured. When the vet, Mike Windwalker, had trudged up here in the middle of the night. When the storm had started a quiet grumbling that now had become almost deafening.

When a message had been left for the vets in the compound? Krystal could understand why Josh might see it that way, but how could a dog's mistreatment be linked to the murder of a man who'd had nothing to do with the dog? That was the only part of this she couldn't add up in some way. Or even Seb's murder. As far as she knew, he and Mason had never even shared a drink.

"Seb didn't know Mason," Krystal volunteered. "I can't imagine any reason both of them should have been murdered."

Connie nodded and scribbled some more in her notebook. "That's interesting. Did they have some kind of problem with one another?"

Krystal shook her head. "Just different people. Seb liked being alone. Mason liked being the center of attention."

Then Connie looked up and asked her last question. "Is there anyone here with a special grudge against Mason Cambridge?"

Krystal couldn't help herself. Even in these horrific times, she couldn't quite govern her sense of humor. "Maybe his editor, but she wasn't here."

Connie almost laughed but managed to maintain a professional demeanor. Krystal could see the humorous glint in her gaze, however. "Should be an easy one" was Connie's answer. "Note that I said *should* and not *will*." Sighing, she shook her head and rose. "You two think of anything else, I wanna hear it. Now back to the emotional mob."

Connie had probably nailed it, Krystal thought. While the room seemed to have calmed overall, people still grew visibly excited when they were questioned. Close to a mob at times.

"I wonder," Josh said, "what they could possibly have to add to this day?"

"Maybe things we didn't see when we were outside."

"Or maybe a whole lot of speculation."

"Like one of us said earlier, that could be fun. And this damn day needs some fun."

Krystal lifted Reject onto a chair beside her and she began to stroke his silky fur. He looked up at her from blue eyes, the adoring eyes that only a dog could have.

"Why do you suppose Reject wanted *me*?" Krystal wondered.

"Who knows? The dog picked you. That ought to be good enough."

She met Josh's gaze and saw warmth there. Warmth after a day from hell. Recalling his brief embrace from earlier, she wished she could just crawl into his arms and seek that feeling of safety again.

As soon as she had the thought, she yanked herself back from it. She was no weakling to depend on anyone for a sense of security. She was strong enough in herself.

Although today had made her wonder a bit. She thought of the time they'd spent out there in that violent storm. Unseen things whipping around hard enough to tear her poncho in a couple of places. Had she felt fear? Uneasiness? Hell, yes. Like when the lightning nearly struck her and Davis. The power out there dwarfed puny humans. But she'd gone out there anyway. Too brave for her own good?

She put her cheek in her hand and just wished for an easy resolution to all of this. Easy and quick.

A chair pulled back at the table and Krystal looked up to see Julia Jansen joining them. Julia painted mostly abstractionist oils. "I thought it was high time to thank the two of you for rescuing me from the storm. I don't know what I'd have done out there on my own. At first I thought it wasn't that bad, but I'm not used to storms this violent."

"Neither am I," Krystal answered. "I kinda feel like Mother Earth is getting even for something."

Julia nodded, dark eyes framed by long dark hair and high cheekbones. "I keep thinking of that creek out there. Imagining how the canyon is bound to flood."

"It probably will, but we've built high enough to be above the flood zone."

Krystal hoped she sounded sure enough to be believable, because the fact was that she couldn't know for certain. Something in the past had carved that canyon. Something violent enough to carry away rocks and carve the steep walls.

Julia sighed, looking weary. "I'm not going to be able to sleep. I'm not sure anyone will, but I don't mind telling you this is scary. Two people dead and no reason for it. And how do we know that a killer or killers aren't getting closer? Or maybe are somewhere in this room?"

Josh spoke kindly. "Hardly likely anyone can get away with another murder in a room this crowded."

Julia appeared to accept what he said, but Krystal didn't believe it. In a crowd it would be easy to knife someone without being spotted.

Her skin had begun to crawl again. She needed to do something. Anything.

Then she spoke quietly, noting a movement that Josh had warned her to pay attention to. "People are breaking up into groups."

Julia drew a sharp breath. "What's that mean?"

Josh swore quietly. "I gotta get around this room and find out why people are dividing."

Krystal shook her head sharply and stood up. "They'll trust me easier than you." She leaned over and briefly squeezed Julia's wrist. "You stay here with Josh. You'll be safe."

The first place Krystal headed was the small group gathered around Darlene Dana. She appeared to be coming down from her earlier shock and spoke only kindly of Mason. Krystal wondered wryly if Mason had been some kind of Jekyll and Hyde, changing personalities when with his agent.

But the conversation seemed benign enough.

The clustering she was finding around the room didn't seem anywhere near as benign. Some of the clusters were trying to pick out people in the room who they mistrusted. People who might be responsible for this terror. Bordering on ugly, hateful and possibly deadly theories.

Then there were the others, much quieter, less conspiracy-minded. Relying on the sheriff and his deputies to take care of the matter. Inclined to feel safer among so many in this room.

Trouble was brewing, she realized, and she didn't know how to control it or slow it down. A conflict between the opposing viewpoints could get ugly.

Making her way back to Josh, she sat at the table. Julia had moved on to talk with Darlene. "It's getting nasty out there. Some people are blowing up conspiracy theories and pointing fingers at others."

Josh nodded. "Knew it couldn't be long. People are freaking predictable."

"So, what can I do? What can *we* do?"

"Establish some kind of control."

"How the hell do we do that?"

"I'm thinking."

Well, she supposed that was a good sign. Josh certainly had to have more experience with this kind of situation. She'd never had one in her life.

"Hell," he said finally, and reached for his walkie. The first person he reached was the sheriff. "Gage? What would you say to me asking some of my guys to come in here? Preemptive crowd control."

Gage's voice crackled in the affirmative. "We've found a few things. Tell you when we get back there. In the meantime, some control would be useful."

Josh ended the call, then stared down at his walkie as if it were a snake. "God, I don't want to ask this of my guys. Do you have any idea how far this could set them back?"

He shook his head, then met Krystal's gaze. "No alternative."

She felt her heart breaking as she looked at this man forced to abandon a goal he'd been fighting for for a long time now. Then he changed the channel on the walkie and put through the call.

"Angus? I need a few volunteers to come into the lodge. The place is loaded with people who are on edge, if you get me. Thanks."

Then he jumped up from the table and headed for the privacy of Joan's office. Once there he looked down at the map, then began rolling it up into a tight tube. "There it goes," he said bitterly. "All that striving, all that trying. Back into the war zone."

Krystal's heart went from breaking to shattering. All those lives about to be wasted again because some idiots in the lodge couldn't be trusted to exercise their own self-control.

But what could she say? When Josh surprised her by pulling her into his arms, she had no doubt which way the comfort was flowing.

She'd give him everything she had.

Chapter Eight

Four of Josh's soldiers appeared at the lodge in about twenty minutes. Three men and a woman who looked as if she could carry any load the guys could. The tromp of their booted feet, in cadence, had brought Krystal and Josh from Joan's office.

The room fell silent, staring in amazement at this unexpected invasion. None of the four carried guns, Krystal noted, but the potential threat was hardly less visible as they stood there in a straight line, at attention, in their camo clothing and ponchos.

One spoke. "Reporting for duty, Colonel."

Josh answered, "Thanks, Angus. I appreciate you all volunteering." Then he looked around at a room that had gone from stunned to whispering. "These soldiers are here to protect you. Even from yourselves. If I were you, I wouldn't want to make it difficult for them to provide that protection."

Joan emerged from the kitchen with Donna Carstairs, her chief cook. "Josh? Okay to offer coffee and food to your soldiers?"

"After today, I'm sure they'd be grateful. At ease, troops."

At once the four soldiers broke from formation and

scattered around the room. The effect was to make them appear less of a threat. Yet people remained wary and startled by their arrival.

Krystal, for her part, was grateful that Mason Cambridge couldn't be here. She could just imagine the story he'd weave around the presence of the soldiers.

But people started to talk. Started to hear that these soldiers, so long hidden behind stockade walls, had emerged to protect them all.

Moods gradually became friendlier.

And some of that ugly talk faded away.

Except, of course, the inevitable wondering about whether a murderer was in this room right now. People kept looking around, aware that a threat could be standing only a few feet away.

Soldiers or not, the situation was explosive.

JOSH WATCHED THE soldiers spread out, helping themselves to food but speaking to no one. He wished he could gather them into a group session right now, to help them over this hump of being surrounded by civilians, the very people who had failed to understand them when they needed it most.

Instead of looking as if they needed some reassurance to get through this trial, however, they'd become stoic, revealing nothing of the inner turmoil they must be experiencing from this exposure.

He walked among them, sharing a few quiet words, thanking them. They all nodded, and at least none of them showed the thousand-yard stare that could have warned of trouble. None of this group of four had disconnected in the least way.

And he thought he felt their gratitude when he added an expression of his pride in the way they were handling the situation.

Carly Narth, whose experience had left her with a scarred face, shrugged. "Gotta do what you gotta do, Colonel."

He watched her turn away, changing the direction of her attention again to the crowd they were keeping an eye on. Carly had a terrible story. A roadside bomb had burned her badly. That had been awful enough, but when she'd come home she'd learned that her own family wouldn't look at her. They couldn't handle her injury and didn't want to.

Nor had the rest of the world been much kinder. It was a wonder she showed her face to anyone anywhere. But in this room, her defiance was almost palpable.

KRYSTAL WAS JUST about reaching the point of sleeping upright while leaning against a wall when the sheriff returned along with two of his deputies.

He pulled his hat off, shaking the hair that had nevertheless managed to get wet despite his rain protection. "We've got the crime areas cordoned off. Nobody gets inside those zones. It's a damn mess. Anyway, we'll be back in the morning with more extensive help and the crime scene unit." He glanced around the room. "You gonna need any extra help here?"

He had to have noted the edginess of the room in one sweep of his gaze.

"At the moment," Josh answered, "I'd say no."

Gage nodded, once again sweeping the room with his dark gaze. "Okay. We're starting to get some comms back, mostly landlines, a few satellite phones, but with a tele-phone tree you ought to be able to reach us from here. Keep people off the internet and off their cells, though."

Josh nodded. "Lousy bandwidth?"

"The lousiest." Gage slapped his hat back on his head and turned to take his deputies from the lodge with him. Then he paused, speaking to the deputy Josh had met earlier. "Connie? You mind hanging around here?"

"Not in the least, boss."

"Just keep me posted."

Then with a sweep, all the deputies but one left the lodge. Connie put her feet up on one table and watched the room over the edge of a coffee cup. She didn't look the least bit weary. And her uniform provided another layer of authority.

Because the room was beginning to seethe again. People were uneasy. Lacking any useful information. Knowing only that terrible things were happening and they were stuck in a virtual cave. No place to run, no place to hide. Faces were growing tighter, more worried. With the sheriff gone there was even less reason for peace.

But the presence of Josh's people in the room seemed to be keeping the cork stuffed in the bottle. As if these seemingly frightened people didn't want to get involved with those hard-eyed veterans. Nor should they.

Reject, who'd been curled up quietly as near as he could get to Krystal, suddenly raised his head, ears perked. He didn't make a sound, not even a growl, but he looked around as if measuring something.

But what?

Josh caught sight of the husky's awareness, too, and

scanned the room, following the dog's gaze. Something wasn't right, and it wasn't right in this room.

But how could that be possible? Damn near everyone had been sitting here all day. A few had left only to return as the lousy weather made remaining alone in their cabins an unattractive option.

But could a murderer really be sitting here among them? The question had crossed Krystal's mind and made her no less uneasy now. But how could anyone tell?

She met Josh's gaze, saw the steeliness returning. He wasn't dismissing the possibility.

But even if the killer was right here with them, how could they know? If one more person fell to the blade of a knife, how could anyone know who the killer was? Too many people.

As awful as this day had been, for the first time Krystal felt a real sense of hopelessness. Then there was Reject. He had become alert, and now he jumped down awkwardly from his chair and began to move from person to person as if seeking a pat. Most obliged him.

Krystal looked at Josh. "Could he smell something?"

"God knows. This day would have probably washed away anything but a pigsty."

He had a point, but Reject continued his trip around the room, accepting tidbits of food when they were offered.

Krystal's gaze slipped to the heavily curtained windows again. A bullet had come through that glass. Aimed at no one, it seemed, but maybe aimed at anyone. And the point of that? To instill more terror? To confuse everything more?

"Hell," she muttered.

Josh looked at her. "What?"

"I'm just wishing we were down closer to Conard City. Surrounded by neighbors, all of whom give a damn and know everything on the grapevine."

One corner of his hard mouth lifted. "You feel like that often?"

"Actually, no," she admitted. "I went to school with a lot of people down there and I can drop in for a visit anytime I want. It's not like I'm any more isolated than I want to be."

"So what's changed?"

She twisted her mouth. "Other than a crazed killer?"

He nodded slowly. "Tell you what. You try to catch some sleep on that couch in your mother's office. I'll keep watch over you."

"That's a generous offer," she answered more warmly than she intended. "But you've got more important things to watch."

He shook his head. "I've got four good helpers, and all of them are going to need to cadge their own sleep in stages. You just take yours now. You'll be more useful."

Useful? she wondered as she headed back to Joan's office. Joan had already claimed the recliner and appeared to be out like a light. Good. She'd been going nonstop since early that morning.

Grabbing a blanket, Krystal curled up on the sofa and wondered if she'd be able to sleep at all.

But she did. It was as if Josh's presence out there lifted some of her worries.

At least for a while.

JOSH KEPT AN eye on the lodge great room, and Krystal, all night. He was used to doing without sleep as long as necessary, and this was one of those nights.

Perplexity troubled him, though. Two people murdered by different methods.

And then, what about Reject? Why would anyone attack that dog? And the bigger question: Who the hell had put a bullet through that window? No one had been out there to do that, had they? At least not from the lodge, as far as he knew. And why? Just to terrorize everyone? Or to cause them to close the curtains and see nothing outside.

That latter thought gave him heartburn. Reduced visibility was a dangerous problem.

How many killers might there be? Who might have been missing in the hours before anyone suspected there had been murders? He was ready to discount the people they had gathered up from their cabins. None of them appeared capable of such killing, although anything was possible.

God. He rubbed his eyes and resumed his study of the room. He noticed his own unit was just as busy watching, even as the clients in the room began to fall asleep with their heads on tables, their bodies spread on area rugs. Filling whatever comfortable chairs they might have found.

The thunder, at least, had finally drawn into the distance. Maybe morning, bringing the sheriff and his experienced teams, would shed light on everything. Maybe they'd even have some *actual* light to see by. Not that he was eager to see any more detail in those two cabins.

He didn't need imagination to fill in what his flashlight beam had missed.

Reject evidently finished his survey of the room, keeping his secrets in the way of a dog, and struggled up onto the chair beside Josh. Josh reached out to pet the animal. Dogs were such wonderful companions that he often thought people didn't deserve them.

He eventually noticed one person who seemed more restless than the others. Mary Collins, wasn't it? A romance novelist who'd been published. Was fear keeping her awake?

Damn, he'd never imagined that he'd get to know any of these people, let alone by name. His whole purpose in being in this area was to provide a refuge and psychological care to vets most in need.

Being a psychologist didn't necessarily give him special insights, but his time in uniform had given him a connection few who had only sat behind desks as professionals could have had.

Maybe he was kidding himself that he was doing these vets of his any particular good. But some at times felt ready to move on, which he counted a victory. Others might never be ready.

Josh never judged them. Judgment was the last thing any of them deserved or needed. They'd know when their own time to leave came.

And right now, this group looked filled with purpose and determination. That had to be a good thing. Maybe. Or it could be slashing old wounds open. No way to guess at this point.

Then his thoughts drifted to Krystal and he closed his eyes briefly. She was the most attractive woman he'd met in years, and it wasn't just her natural beauty. Her intelligence. Her courage. She'd insisted on going out with him into that storm earlier, even knowing the possible dangers they faced.

It was the kind of behavior he expected from women in uniform, not from quiet, inexperienced civilians who weren't on a steroid rush.

Krystal embodied a lot of things he admired. And felt attracted to.

And he was wasting his time daydreaming. He'd chosen his path in life, an important one, and he wasn't about to start shredding it. Too many people relied on him.

Their faces floated before his mind's eye, faces that he'd come to know well for the most part. Faces that hid the unending internal battles they fought. He couldn't possibly tear that group apart in pursuit of selfish ends.

All of it was pipe dreaming anyway. They had a much more immediate issue to deal with: murders. One or two perpetrators? The idea of a single killer seriously bothered him, given the difference in the crimes, and he wondered if he could possibly get some of Gage's impressions about the murders. Although he'd learned cops were pretty silent about ongoing investigations, there was always the hope Gage might be of a different mind under these circumstances.

But then morning brought a new list of troubles. Of course, these artists wanted to get back to their cabins for their computers, for a change of clothes. For some semblance of normal life.

And of course, they started convincing themselves the threat had passed. No more murders so far. A great metric. Not.

Josh drew a steadying breath and began to make plans for a new problem, one that at least probably had the sense to wait until after Joan had served breakfast. Then this crowd would try to move out.

LYING IN THE middle of the room, Mary Collins thought about how easy she had found it to locate a coconspirator in the murder of Mason Cambridge. Enough people around here hated the man with a purple passion.

But only Mel Marbly had a desire as strong as her own to end the existence of Cambridge. Mason had spent a lot of time insulting Mel Marbly about his gardening work. Called him a dirt pusher, a mud rat, a stupid sod farmer. Criticized him constantly for dirt under his fingernails. Called him a dolt.

More insults than any man should have to take and Mel had been taking those shots for years now. It was as if Mason Cambridge needed to look down on anyone who actually worked with their hands. And somehow Mason had managed not to toss his insults when the Metcalfes were around, and Mel hadn't complained to them.

But Mary had heard. The whole thing disgusted her until her stomach turned over every time she heard Mason. She'd often seen hate glowing in Brady Marbly's eyes as well. Perhaps more than her husband Mel's.

But Mary knew neither Brady's nor Mel's feelings of rage for the insults they'd endured could come close to her own feelings of hatred. Her *justified* feelings of hatred.

For Mason had stolen from her. Had taken her dreams and claimed credit for them. Had used them to launch a career that should have been her own.

Mary hadn't stopped seething in years. The calmer voices of friends, who reminded her that ideas couldn't be copyrighted, made her feel no better. Reminders that a book never would have been written since Shakespeare if no ideas could be copied helped Mary not at all.

None of it meant a thing to her. Vengeance meant everything and that man deserved to pay for treating her like dust beneath his heels. She hadn't mattered to him, not even enough to give her credit for her ideas.

She'd been useful. Nothing more. Catapulting him to a career as a bestseller when he stole her idea, leaving her nothing but life as a mid-list romance novelist.

Because even though her ideas were better than Mason's, they got brushed aside by publishers because Mason was going to do it better. Or maybe not so much better, but he was guaranteed huge sales.

Right. He'd stolen her chance and wouldn't give even part of it back to her.

But Mel was serving her well. He'd wanted to kill Mason, but he'd decided to stab Sebastian to death to make it look like a different kind of crime. Then the bullet through the window at that damn dog. A brilliant touch, if she did say so herself, although she feared Mel was getting his own ideas, might mess things up. Too many victims. Too many possibilities now. Would that cause confusion or lead the cops right to Mel?

She hated dogs, but this one had become a freaking nuisance. He was next on her list if Mel didn't mess things up. Still, she needed to find a private minute with Mel in order to make sure he was still largely in line with her. Especially since he wounded the damn dog in the first place, without clearing it with her. Still, it had proved to be a touch that had added to the terror. Maybe not a mistake on Mel's part. She still hadn't made up her mind about Sebastian, much as his murder must be muddying the waters.

But Mel was beginning to make her seriously uneasy.

In the meantime, she sat back, pretending occasionally to join the general fear, and just enjoyed all that she had unleashed. She hadn't expected quite this much uproar over one dead author.

She should have guessed. Mason would do everything in the biggest way possible, even die. But never had she guessed that she could enjoy the reaction to his murder as much as his murder itself. Life *did* offer some gifts, few though they were.

Then she looked at the soldiers, including that one who had appeared to be in charge. She hadn't expected them. Since a year ago when the stockade had started to be built, she had known they liked to be left alone. They wanted no part of the rest of the world except the two or three who occasionally went shopping for essentials in Conard City.

Now they were out and about, at least some of them, and they made her skin crawl. Unpredictable creeps, likely to explode into violence without warning. Wasn't that what these PTSD guys did?

Even the sheriff and his jerks didn't worry her as much. Then she forced her attention away, for fear she might draw notice by focusing too much. She had more important matters to deal with anyway. Much more important.

Like making sure she took care of the Marblys before they could talk. Then to get out of here unscathed.

She had confidence in her abilities to escape. After all, look what Mason had achieved just because of her. *Mary* was the one with the brilliant, devious mind.

She ordered another coffee and half dozed as she watched the room. Not long before something would start happening, she felt. The only question was whether she should take advantage of it just yet.

THE COMPOSITION OF the room started to change as the few remaining deputies, cold and exhausted from a long night in the rain, began to rotate through to take advantage of the hot coffee and sweet rolls Joan and her staff provided.

As near as Krystal could tell, the crime scene units were out at the cabins, but no information could be shared yet.

The room did calm, however, as if the growing desire to escape eased, at least for now. As if the presence of those uniformed deputies changed the mental landscape. Even those who had been talking of returning to their own cabins decided to delay in favor of coffee and rolls.

Josh's soldiers switched off duty then, too. Grabbing something to eat, then heading out, four more to follow them into the lodge.

When Krystal had the chance for a quiet word with Josh, she murmured, "I thought these guys didn't want to be out here with us."

"They don't. But they feel a duty."

In those few words he offered a flood of information. Krystal studied the soldiers with new respect, noting for the first time how many of them were visibly injured. Regardless, they all showed backbones of steel.

"What exactly do you do for them?"

"I'm a psychologist. I'm also a veteran."

Another few words containing a flood of information. And for the first time he shared with her his purpose. His meaning. More than just providing a sanctuary for the wounded.

Her respect for him deepened. This task of his was momentous.

But what had she done with her own life? Dabble at a novel? Help run this writers' retreat, some of which managed to seem awfully indulgent. Although she had to admit her own indulgence in her private little cottage on the creek canyon. Sure, she had duties at the lodge, primarily helping her mother and the staff, but what else of importance did she accomplish?

Hours of scribbling a few words on an otherwise empty computer screen.

"Write anything at all," Davis Daniels had suggested. That didn't seem to work well for her. She needed something more organized to focus on.

Hah! Maybe she should start at the middle or the end of a story and see where that got her. When she'd first started writing, that had been a problem for her: a vivid beginning, then the end too clear not to write immediately, both of them surrounding a big, gaping hole she couldn't figure out how to fill. Some part of her simply felt the story was completed even though it clearly wasn't.

She'd had a lot of those false starts in her bottom drawer until she'd finally thrown them on her fireplace. No point in keeping useless ideas.

But sometimes she missed them because they had been so much fun to write. So absorbing they'd carried her totally away.

She was having no such luck this time. Rising, she went to help Joan and the kitchen staff churn out enough food for a suddenly hungry army. The night's storm had begun to drift away, letting patches of sunlight through, and only the dripping of rain from the leaves remained as a reminder.

Even some of the curtains had been drawn open to let in the freshening light. People avoided the open ones, which was kind of ridiculous to Krystal's way of thinking, given that she suspected a whole lot of them were wanting to get back to their cabins, which would expose them far more than the windows.

The urge to return to private cabins grew even stronger when Angus MacDougall and Josh climbed up to the roof to realign the satellite dish. After a few false starts, computers came on again, and people started using their cell phones and satellite phones.

The world had returned to normal.

Except for two corpses lying out there. Except for the inescapable presence of one or two murderers.

Yeah, normal, Krystal thought. Not the kind of normal any of them should want.

THE COPS WEREN'T off duty, however. As they warmed up and ate, they moved among the residents, talking quietly, explaining that, at this time, the other cabins appeared safe.

"No signs of breaking and entering," Krystal heard more than one of them say. "But that doesn't necessarily mean there can't be."

Uneasy looks passed around the room, then the remaining poet, Paul Aston of the crazy hair, raised his voice. "Then just what the hell are we supposed to do, Deputy? Hang around here all day with no good reason? We have *work*."

Sheriff Gage Dalton had come into the room unseen,

but when he lifted his voice he claimed everyone's attention. "Stick it out a few more hours," he said firmly. "You don't know what's out there and why this happened. But if you really want to race out there by yourselves, be my guest. I can't stop you. Just stay away from the areas marked off with yellow crime scene tape." He stepped outside, probably to speak to some of his deputies.

Well, that dampened the growing restlessness, although probably only temporarily. At some point these people were going to honestly decide the threat was over. That someone had a grudge against Mason Cambridge, easily understandable, and Sebastian Elsin had just gotten in the way of a vendetta.

It sure made more sense than any other explanation.

But what were they going to find when they got out there?

DARLENE, MASON'S AGENT, was having the hardest time of anyone. That, too, was understandable. She'd found the body. That alone would have seriously shaken anyone to the core. But to have it be the body of someone she knew well? Far worse.

Darlene didn't seem to want any physical comfort, not a hug or a pat on the shoulder. She remained curled up in a padded chair, wrapped in a blanket and sipping hot chocolate whenever Joan, Krystal or the staff thought to bring it to her. And her hands had never stopped shaking, most especially when Connie had interviewed her about what she had seen.

The woman needed an ambulance, Krystal thought, but getting one up here right now seemed difficult. Mud and more mud layered the road outside, and then came the first low rumble. Landslide. Inevitable. Krystal prayed it would remain in the confines of the canyon, where it would do less harm. Usually such floods did, although they could make a mess of the canyon for a while.

"Okay," Gage Dalton announced as he reappeared, grabbing all the attention in the room. "It's a mess out there. You've already been told it's bad, but now we have landslides. I have no way of knowing how long they'll last or how bad they'll be. If anyone here decides to venture out, then you'd better take someone with you. I'd prefer you didn't, though. I'm having to bring up a lot of heavy-duty equipment from the county, and from neighboring counties as well, and we're going to need some of it at lower elevations."

He paused, looking around, clearly gauging the responses. "You go out there on your own, you're going to *be* on your own. I don't have the manpower to dig you all out."

Krystal shuddered. Frankly, she couldn't imagine much worse than being buried alive in mud. Inevitably, she looked toward the porch windows and wondered if they'd hold against an onslaught, especially the one with the bullet hole in it.

But the impatient swirling in the room had started to settle down again, and Krystal had reached the end of her rope. Using her jacket as a pillow, she gathered it up and used it on the table as a place to rest her head. For a little while, she woke occasionally as if she couldn't quite rest with all the people around, but at last sleep claimed her in a deep embrace.

Dreams of Josh followed her, however. Dreams of the confident way he moved, the force in his voice when it was needed, his surprising gentleness with his vets.

Hard and soft. She liked both.

Chapter Nine

Josh kept an eye on Krystal as she slept bent over the table, thinking she was going to ache like hell when she woke.

But he had other concerns running alongside thoughts of her. Sheriff Dalton was of the opinion that the landslides were pretty much stopping. He sent some of his Humvees out to check and they came back with reasonably good news.

Which left the crowd in the lodge great room. Their urge to get out of the place was growing by the minute. But what would they find when they got out there?

Then Angus appeared, radio in hand. "How much help you want?"

"How much you got?"

"Damn near everybody. Any of their reticence has vanished."

Of course it had, Josh thought. The kind of emergency these people had trained for, had faced for so many years. They knew what to do in this situation and right now needed no plans or directions for the unknowns of the civilian world.

This could also throw them back into their personal hells, but Josh couldn't bring himself to deprive these men and women of their renewed sense of purpose.

He suggested, "They want to escort people back to their

cabins? Because there's no guarantee these artists will be able to find them easily after this storm. Paths washed away and so on. But our troops found them all last night and a look at the map will be all they need for guidance. Plus, the residents have to be provisioned if they want to stay."

"You know we can carry the provisions, except the most disabled among us. Just get the crap together."

Joan was happy to open her larder. The food had been meant for these people anyway.

It was settled. Part of Josh even felt good about it. His people out there helping these artists hike safely home would create a more tolerant environment for them all. A win-win. Maybe.

Of course, as life had taught him, anything could get worse.

THE ARTISTS PROVED initially surprised that soldiers in camo ponchos, carrying heavy packs, insisted on accompanying them to their cabins. Some wanted to object out of mistrust, but most quickly saw the advantage in it. Some even managed to offer their thanks.

Still, the stone-faced soldiers who accompanied each of them were intimidating. Nor did they appear to have any desire not to be. They marched out with their charges and they looked ready to handle anything.

Krystal sat up, rubbing her eyes, and having missed the departures, she took a belated trip to the kitchen to find out if she could help. The small staff seemed to be doing all right and assured her they'd taken shifts to sleep. That left Joan, who looked as if she hadn't slept a wink.

"Mom, you can let me take over for a little while. You need some sleep."

Joan put her head in her hands. "Do you know what this is going to do to us? To the business?"

That had been the farthest thing from Krystal's mind, but considering how much of her effort, time and life Joan had put into this retreat, Krystal could understand her mother's concern. Or maybe it was a partial concern, unwilling to deal with the murder issue.

"We'll come back," Krystal hastened to assure Joan. "Awful as this is, it's a single incident out of years of success."

"Right." Joan rubbed her eyes. "Guess what headline is going to follow us."

"Headlines don't last long."

"But they can be brought up at every opportunity on the internet. Nothing ever dies anymore." Then Joan closed her eyes. "Except people," she murmured. "Except people. Mason I can almost understand, but Sebastian? He practically faded into the background."

Krystal leaned back in her chair, knowing her mother was right, but not knowing what she could say about it. Sebastian couldn't have been any more inoffensive. Who could have a grudge against him?

The question gave her a renewed chill. Cops and soldiers notwithstanding, something was very wrong out there. Terribly wrong. And Krystal couldn't be sure they had enough protection to deal with a sick grudge of some kind. How many people would it take to turn this entire lodge into a deadly fishbowl? She'd bet not very many.

JOSH'S MIND WAS running along a similar but different track. He and the sheriff were hitting it off well, sharing as much information as they could, but it wasn't a whole lot. They staked out coordinates on the map, presuming the killer or killers must still be out there, but neither of them quite believing it.

"Two killers," Gage decided.

Josh agreed. "Methods too different."

"But why?" Gage spoke the question that neither of them could answer. Why two murderers?

The sight of his soldiers marching out with civilians, determined to protect them, filled Josh with pride. Not all chose to go with the civilians but he could understand what this might be costing them whether they chose to remain behind or take the dangerous trek. Memories. Horrors. Risks to themselves and friends.

A trek that could be more dangerous in many ways. He wished he could go out with them, but they were separated, one soldier to two civilians, and he'd be useless.

So he stayed at the lodge, patrolling outside. Reject, that tough little husky, limped with him everywhere but gave no signs of concern. That much was good, anyway.

Even though the rain had stopped and patches of blue sky showed between the trees, leaves still dripped water, a constant patter. Then every so often came a rumble in the distance. More mountain sliding? He hoped the trees would be able to withstand most of it.

The heavy equipment Gage Dalton had promised began to arrive, although exactly what it was supposed to do at this point beat Josh. Maybe just stand at the ready in case a dangerous slide happened.

Josh's own experience of such things had been mostly limited to drier terrain, although Afghanistan was by no means a dry country for the most part. But rains like yesterday? A whole different ball of wax.

He took a few minutes to check on Krystal and her mother. They looked about as depressed as two people could. Well, they were watching a life's work be washed away and murdered away. He could get it.

As if the situation wasn't bad enough all by itself, regardless of the future.

Two murders, so very different. That was bugging the hell out of him. There had to be a point. Not just that two murderers might be involved, but that the crimes had been staged to be so different. A message there? He and Gage were left scratching their heads.

And did Reject fit in somehow? He glanced at the fluffy husky and couldn't imagine it. Yet the dog had been seriously injured, then dumped as if he were some kind of message at the stockade.

No sense in any of it.

Given his background, Josh didn't necessarily need things to make sense. War sure as hell rarely did. Act and react. Except right now there was little to react to.

Two bodies, ostensibly being pored over by a crime scene unit. Two bodies unrelated except they were both clients of the retreat.

Two bodies, making no sense at all. Nor did patrolling the outside of the retreat lodge. Gage had as many deputies as he could spare, and while they hardly created an impenetrable wall, neither did Josh's men and women.

Nothing could protect totally.

Hell. He went inside with Reject, sure the dog would cheer Krystal at least a bit. He'd noticed how that animal managed to bring small smiles to her face.

Although very few of the original crowd remained in the great room of the lodge, they were making use of the kitchen staff and waitpersons, who appeared to be glad to be occupied.

Who wouldn't be right now, Josh wondered. The ugliness of this whole situation carried him back into times he would much rather forget. Times when those he'd cared about had paid the price of war. When Carly Narth had become too wounded to join so-called polite society again. He remembered that awful scene all the way to his gut.

Limbs had been lost. Men and women had been crippled. And for some of them, prosthetics provided no answer.

Then there were the spouses who could no longer take the changes in their husbands and wives. Those who feared having them around their children. The ultimate rejection.

God, he hated to think about it. Hated that he could do only small bits for people so terribly wounded.

But Krystal looked happy to see Reject and that made him feel somewhat better. He was coming to care for Krystal as much as he cared for his own people. He could see she was going through hell right now, but it was more than that. He admired her innate strength she seemed so unwilling to let go of.

Where had that come from? Did it matter? She stroked Reject, who decided to give her his belly, a true honor. Poor little doggie with a cast on his leg and two legs splinted. So badly mistreated by some human. But then, humans had a way of doing that. Bitterness crept into his thoughts, an unwanted visitor. He shoved it away, burying it in a deep place he never wanted to visit again.

He didn't like the sight of the deputies wandering in the woods, seeking scattered clues. On all those police vests yellow showed out like a target. A protection from accidental misfires by fellow deputies but a damn bright announcement to anyone out there who wanted a target.

He pulled on his poncho again, making sure his KA-BAR was firmly tucked into its sheath. In his hands that knife was just about as good as a pistol. Or a rifle. He could throw with enviable accuracy.

But to get outside again, that was important. To keep an eye on those deputies who announced their presence. In his camo he could remain damn near invisible and so could the people of his unit.

He paused, giving Krystal a kiss on her cheek that obviously surprised her. Hell, it surprised him, too, as did the instant flood of desire that slammed him. God, not now. "I'm going out for a little while. Don't worry."

She eyed him up and down, and the faintest of smiles edged her face. "You'll be invisible out there?"

"That's my hope. Plenty of practice."

Joan didn't look any happier about his foray but offered no objection, as if she knew a protest would be wasted. Evidently she got it.

Rain still dripped from leaves, recreating the sound of the storm that had just passed. The ground was a mess of runnels, and washed rivers of pine needles and leaves. Useless for tracking.

But maybe not everything was. Tree limbs had snapped at a man's height, too low for the wildness of the storm. Some had broken even lower. Stealthy this guy was not.

Yet what real purpose could he feel in killing two so unrelated people? Mason he could understand. Damn near everyone at the retreat understood that one, but Sebastian? No one appeared to even speculate about that.

So what was the link? There had to be one beyond a rental at this retreat.

Those who remained at the lodge great room appeared as unhappy as those who had left. People who had determined they must work even in the face of such threat.

Hell. One more round of the wide porch, one more check on the deputies he could pick out, then he returned to the lodge to sit with Krystal and Joan. Two people who needed reassurance. Two people for whom he had none to offer.

Joan brightened a little as he joined them. Krystal's face was a bit gloomier, but not entirely. She managed a faint smile.

"What now?" Krystal asked bluntly. "There's no way to come back from two murders. None."

Joan sighed and the brief brightness she had shared abruptly vanished. "Screwed by the internet."

Josh, gathering their meaning was about their business, couldn't exactly argue that. He already had some experience of what a few typed lines on a social media note could do. Didn't matter if they were malicious. They just had to be personal in a way that revealed secrets anyone ought to be able to keep.

Privacy. Crap. No longer possible.

But he looked at Joan and tried to find some way to reassure her. Even the slightest thing.

Then a thing, a small thing, occurred to him. He pulled out his cell phone.

Joan drew a sharp breath. "The cells are working again?"

Josh shook his head sharply. "Sat phones only, and intermittent at that. Angus is out there with a deputy trying to get it all up and running. Anyway, this is on my phone, not a signal. I want you to see this."

Then with a flip he ran through photos until he came to the one he wanted. "This is Carly Narth. One of my best soldiers. And you can imagine what she's been through, thanks to the internet."

And there, unmistakably, was Carly's horribly scarred face, a testimony to the atrocities of war. A testimony to man's inhumanity to men.

"Oh my God," Joan breathed. Krystal bit her lip and seemed to stop breathing.

Joan raised her horrified gaze. "What can she do?"

Josh flipped his phone away from the photo and shoved it into his pocket. "What *can* she do?"

Krystal shook her head. "I saw her last night but I never dreamed she'd been injured so badly. She kept her face turned away or under her poncho hood. My God, Josh. How do you ever live with that?"

Josh simply shook his head. "Her family couldn't. Threw her out. Too upsetting for the children. *Her* children, I might add."

"How could they…" Krystal's voice trailed off.

"Because they *could*," Josh said harshly. "Because social services workers agreed that it was too awful for the kids to live with. Never mind that their mother is a hero. Evidently that doesn't count."

The women exchanged looks, small nods. Krystal faced him. "You're telling us something."

"Damn straight. Carly never gave up. She's still fighting for a normal life despite her appearance. She's going to make it, too. But what about the two of you? You gonna fight or are you gonna give up?"

He had no doubt of their answer, not after seeing Carly, but how long would they stick to it? "Anyway," he continued almost harshly, "you can give yourselves excuses or you can fight. I suggest fighting, and that starts with the damn internet. Sure, anyone can find out about you if they want to, but the question becomes who is going to bother. After these murders pass, nobody is going to care since you're not involved. Sure, there'll be a brief flurry of Mason's books on the shelves because he's dead, but that won't make much of a difference. He was a lousy writer anyway. People read him only because they ran out of other horror writers to read."

Krystal smiled. "You've read him?"

"Much to my embarrassment. He was awful, always awful, and he was coattailing on someone else's work if you want my opinion."

Mary Collins had been listening, and now she sat upright, trying not to be obvious about it. So others agreed with her about the theft of her work. That Mason had made it only because of her.

Joan sighed heavily. "You're saying to just ignore this. And Mason."

"It won't be easy at first. Reporters will be everywhere. Nightly news will want to see you. Thing is, don't give them what they want. They want shock. No way. I'll help you with figuring that out."

Krystal surprised him by reaching across the table to lay her hand on his. "You've had to go through this."

"Damn straight. More than once. I'll help."

MARY COLLINS FELT a strong urge to get rid of Josh just then. She didn't want Mason to get away with any of his misdeeds. None. Getting even with this retreat was part of her plan, too. After all, they'd made Mason a star guest for years.

"Damn it all to hell," she muttered under her breath. This damn soldier was going to be a pain in her butt.

She knew she could shoot a man. She'd gone with Mel to make sure they took out Mason. She hadn't anticipated Sebastian's murder, though. However, Mel Marbly had proved useful in taking out Sebastian—although he'd been a lot messier about the job—and helped create a distraction, for which Mary forgave him for getting his own ideas. Of course, thinking about this caused Mary a small smile. Clearly Mel had enjoyed Sebastian's killing, and had certainly made it different enough from Mason's murder.

Unfortunately, she'd have to get rid of Mel now, and maybe his wife as well. Still, given a little time, she could get out of here before two more murders were uncovered. Murders she couldn't possibly be linked to.

Still hiding a smile, she sipped fresh coffee and played solitaire. Across the room she could clearly see the damn Metcalfes alone with Josh Healey.

She hoped the Metcalfes' business suffered a setback, but Josh Healey was a different concern. She hadn't planned on his unit emerging from behind their walls to get involved in any of this. From everything she'd heard about them, they never showed their faces except for one or two guys driving into town for supplies.

No, she hadn't planned on them guarding this place, hunting for killers.

She swore silently again, but then realized these guys wouldn't be hard to take care of. No, from what little she'd heard, they didn't like to be out of their stockade. Given a small opportunity, they'd head back to their hideout.

A bunch of sickos.

Satisfied, she flipped another card in her deck.

She'd get 'em all. Every damn one of them. She was smart enough to plan all of this.

Chapter Ten

Josh noticed that Reject never entirely slept. All the while he appeared to be snoozing, his ears never stopped perking, twisting. He was listening every single moment.

Josh couldn't have asked for a better guard. He'd seen what K-9s could do in the military, knew how alert they could be to sounds and smells. Reject apparently had the same instincts.

Which meant Josh didn't hesitate to send Joan to her bedroom and Krystal to a spare room. He swore to them that Reject would warn them of anything, and recalling the husky's attention to the window and his growling just before the gunshot, they believed him.

But Krystal was a different matter. Somehow he followed her into her small, private room. Somehow she turned into him, surrounding him with her arms, drawing him into a snug embrace. He closed his eyes, trying to remember the last time a woman had made him feel this way.

Sadly, he couldn't. Other women had passed through his life, but Krystal was unique.

He could no more have stopped himself than he could have stopped an incoming missile. He wrapped his own arms around her and held her as snugly as he dared. Bent his head and risked a kiss of her soft, warm lips.

Heard the sigh escape her. Felt her move even closer into his arms. "Oh, Josh," she murmured.

His head nearly exploded with desire. God, he wanted her. His entire body flamed for her. A throbbing drove him toward completion, ignoring the clothes between them, ignoring every impediment.

Then he heard Gage's roughened voice from the great room.

At once he leaned back. Krystal, too, leaned back.

"Damn," he muttered. Then, "Soon. I promise." It was a promise that would require more than the threat stalking them now for him to break. A promise nothing could keep him from fulfilling at the first opportunity.

Reluctantly, he left Krystal. Gage was looking for the murderers and couldn't be ignored. Not even for the heat of desire.

He stepped out of the back room. A few people still sat around tables, that Mary woman playing endless rounds of solitaire.

Not everyone felt safe with cops and soldiers roaming the area.

Gage waved him over and Josh soon bent his head close to the sheriff's. "CSU found something," he murmured. "A woman's small boot print. Nothing like that agent was wearing."

Josh glanced over at Darlene Dana, Mason's agent. The woman seemed to have taken up permanent residence on a sofa, still staring blindly at her mental image of what she had seen when she found Mason. "You got impressions?" Of the shoe pattern. Could be the most useful thing of all.

Gage nodded. "Believe it or not. Rain helped some."

Josh rubbed his chin, thinking. "Okay. I'm not sure

how we'll start a shoe hunt, though. And can you be sure it's a woman's print?"

"Smaller than most men's, although not impossible. Thing is, the tech doesn't think the person could be very heavy, not in that mud."

"But still possibly a small male."

Gage simply shook his head. "Not easy. Never thought this case would be. Hell's bells. Two murders and every sign that they were committed by different people. Find me a reason for that, Josh. Any reason will do at this point."

Josh sighed, frustrated beyond belief. "Nobody's told me a useful thing except about Mason Cambridge. Maybe I should look into this Sebastian Elsin some more. People seem to think he was pretty invisible. Then there's Paul Aston, another poet. Maybe he knows something more about Elsin."

Gage nodded. "I'm about to get truly shorthanded. A lot of folks downstream of these mountains are running into major trouble. They need us."

Josh understood perfectly. "I'll try to keep my unit out here as long as I can. But this situation is hell for them."

"I'm surprised they showed up. Well—" Gage slammed his hat on his head "—I'll keep you posted as I can. Sure would be nice to have full comms back, though. Although we're doing better, up here at least."

Josh couldn't have agreed more.

He looked around the room and finally caught sight of Paul Aston over in a far corner, working on a computer with what had to be a lousy internet connection, especially with comms still unreliable. Hah. Josh remembered the days when an internet connection hadn't been required for the use of a computer. Fancy typing machines for the most part. Boy, had that been a long time ago. He probably shouldn't advertise his age.

He wended his way to the other side of the room and without an apology sat with Aston. Paul looked up, startled by the interruption. "What…?"

"I need a word or two about Sebastian, if you don't mind. Sheriff is curious."

Paul hesitated only a minute before closing the laptop. "I didn't know him very well. Most people didn't."

"But you're both poets, right?"

Paul's smile was crooked. "And we're all humans sharing the same planet, right? About the same relationship."

Josh shook his head, managing an amused shrug. "Can't blame a guy for trying."

"Of course not." Paul leaned forward, elbows on the table. "So, Sebastian. What did I know about him? Give me a minute. It's not like I keep notes on everyone I meet here."

Josh was glad to give him the time. He accepted fresh coffee from Donna Carstairs, who worked out of the kitchen and was apparently doubling as a waitress. "Something to eat?" she asked. "Even a guy like you has to eat sometime."

"What's on the menu?"

"Burgers and more burgers. My second line cook bailed yesterday. Oh, yeah, I think I can make some fries, but it'll take time to heat the deep-fat fryer."

"Then just the burgers, please. Two of them. Mustard and ketchup."

"Ah, a man with my tastes. What about you, Paul?"

"Just some of those wheat crackers if you have them, with some cheese. Not very hungry."

Donna moved on, leaving Josh and Paul alone at the table.

"Okay," Paul continued, "Sebastian. Total introvert, worse than me. But sometimes he'd try to be humorous."

"Tried to be?"

Paul shook his head. "I don't know where he learned to be funny, but a lot of people around here didn't take it that way. Offensive, like. Anyway, it was only once in a while, kinda like he figured out he wasn't making anyone laugh."

That was worth noting, Josh thought, making a mental note.

"Anything else?"

"A bit of a misogynist." Paul sighed. "Not so terribly overt that it couldn't be ignored much of the time, but it was still there, and these days women notice it."

"As well they should," Josh answered.

Paul gave him a half smile. "I imagine you've served with women who wouldn't stand for a bit of it. Anyway, like I said, he mostly soft-pedaled it except with a rare joke that wasn't terribly funny to anyone, except some of the jerkier guys."

Josh lifted a brow, amused in spite of himself. "Jerkier guys?"

Paul sighed. "I'm sure you know exactly the type I mean. Mason led the lot. Thought women existed to serve his needs, treated 'em like they were beneath him. Jerkier than most, but he got away with it, the holy and almighty Mason Cambridge. Those same women hung on his every word."

"I guess you didn't like him either."

Paul just shook his head. "Best to start with a little respect for others. I don't think that man ever felt any."

Donna put two burgers in front of Josh, buns looking a bit stale, burgers more gray than brown. The second plate held Paul's cheese and crackers. "Sorry," she said. "Stove isn't heating up well. Maybe low on propane. Anyway, I promise I can do a better burger than that."

"These are good enough," Josh told her. "If I got picky, I wouldn't have made it all those years in uniform."

Donna flashed a grin. "It'd be nice if everyone else felt the same way. Well, I'm off to see what I got left to do."

Individual soldiers guiding people back to their cabins had worked, at least enough to cut the crowd in the dining room by two-thirds, or so it appeared to Josh as he scanned the area. It struck him that an awful lot of people had somehow decided they weren't at risk from the killer or killers.

How had they managed that? As if he didn't know. How many patrols had he led into death-defying situations with young people who believed they were somehow invincible?

Until the first bloody fight, anyway. Seeing your buddy blown into a cloud of blood and detached limbs had quite a sobering effect. Eighteen-year-olds became men overnight, not always in a good way.

So a lot of these artists had convinced themselves of their own invincibility. That only Mason and Sebastian had been targets—never mind that bullet through the window. Nothing had happened in hours, and that was all they needed to persuade themselves of their own safety. He knew his people would check out the cabins and surrounding areas, but that was no proof against a lurking killer. No way. A single man or woman could slip through those woods unseen if they knew how.

Trying not to grind his teeth because all that ever did was give him a headache, Josh left Paul to his work and began to slowly make his way around the room. Fewer people, easier task, and apparently his frequent appearances at the lodge had eased the fear of him.

Most of it, anyway. Some uneasy looks still darted his way, but then some of them were directed toward Reject. Apparently the dog's preternatural senses yesterday had made him a thing that wasn't quite earthly.

Which could be half-true, Josh thought with mild amusement.

Krystal fell into step beside him before he'd wound his way through half the room.

"People are foolish," she remarked and didn't try to keep her voice down. "I can't believe how many people went back to their cabins. Like making themselves offerings to a killer in the woods."

He didn't disagree, but there was no way to agree with her when others could hear. "My people will check out their security."

"I'm sure they will. But since they don't have Reject's senses, they could miss a lot. Crap."

He glanced at her, reading the strong annoyance in her face. "Cops all over the place, too."

"Not enough of them." She shook her head and came to a dead halt. "They can't *know* they're not out there with a beast who just wants to kill for the joy of it. They can't know that, Josh."

He sighed quietly and looked around, thinking about

the scene differently. "Maybe people started to feel like fish in a bowl. Easier to attack while gathered here."

"We mentioned that, didn't we? I hate to say you're probably right. God, *Mom's* right. She's worried about people getting killed—she's not some kind of monster—but she's also worried about what this can do to the business. Sheesh, Josh, she's spent decades turning this place into a reputable artists' retreat. This'll kill it. Make it visibly unsafe. A kind of reputation you can't claw back, not with the internet."

Josh had no counterargument for that. He'd already said all he could on the subject.

"We'll probably attract the thrill seekers now."

He asked dryly, "The Mason Cambridges you mean?"

At last a smile tickled the corners of her mouth. "Maybe so. But I'm not sure we want to be a retreat for wannabe horror writers, at least not mainly. Damn, we used to have such a nice, peaceful environment."

"It'll come back. It might just take some time." He spoke with more surety than he felt, however. He had only to look at his group of soldiers to know how long bad publicity could last.

Krystal stopped walking and faced him. Their eyes met, and Josh felt an overwhelming *zing* of attraction for her. In an instant he wanted to pull her away to a private place and discover every inch of that body she concealed beneath jeans and loose Western shirts.

Because he was sure it was a perfect body. Even in loose clothing she couldn't hide it all when she moved. But it wasn't just her body.

He wanted her to smile at him. Sigh at him. Murmur his name. Share that strong inner core of hers, one he felt matched his own. A woman to meet him as an equal. A true partner.

He caught himself just before he did something stupid. He didn't want to offend her, and he certainly didn't want to draw attention to her and the way he was feeling about her.

But did he see, in those blue eyes of hers, an answering heat? He could only hope because the time for any of this frankly sucked.

She shook her head a bit, as if in answer to some internal discussion of her own, then faced forward, making it clear she intended to continue the survey of their remaining guests.

She was better at it, too, maybe because the clients here knew her, unlike him. Even though he'd had a highly visible profile here since yesterday, he was still the unknown. A pretty large unknown, he admitted to himself. One of his nicknames in the Army had been Giant. Total exaggeration, but it had given him some idea of how he appeared to others.

Krystal slipped easily into chairs at occupied tables, greeted warmly by everyone. Josh stood back, creating space for her and the people she needed to talk with. When it seemed wise, he seated himself nearby.

Krystal, he discovered, experienced no hesitation about coming right to the point.

"We've had two murders," she said bluntly. "Very different murders. I know the cops interviewed you yesterday, but this is today, guys. I want to know if you remembered something in the meantime. Some little thing that didn't seem important enough to bring up yesterday."

Well, she certainly got the four people she was with to

exchange looks. He didn't get their names. Didn't matter. If they needed them for some reason later, Krystal would know.

"Well," said one of the women slowly, "I thought it was weird how Mason started that creepy story before his murder. Were you listening, Krystal?"

Krystal gave a half shake of her head. "I was busy."

"We *all* should have been," said one of the men.

"I hate to admit it," the woman said, "but that man could spin quite a tale. Anyway, a couple nights before he was killed…didn't you notice it? Sebastian mentioned it at the time." Then she paused, shaking her head, a tear running down her cheek. "Poor Sebastian. He didn't deserve what happened."

Who does? Josh thought a trifle sourly.

The woman dabbed at her eyes. "Anyway, we were sitting there listening to Mason tell his tale and Sebastian turned to me and said, 'Carrie? Doesn't it sound like he's plotting his next book? His next murder?'"

Carrie shuddered. "At the time I thought it was amusing. Of course that's what Mason was doing. He was always doing that. But that night I could only joke that the only thing missing from his story were the fools who ran out into the night woods, instead of staying safely inside, only to meet the killer with the axe. Like all those movies." Carrie shuddered again. "It was exactly like that." She raised a watery gaze to Krystal. "Is it possible he planned his own murder?"

Josh stiffened. He saw a small shudder run down Krystal's back.

"Hardly likely," Krystal answered firmly. "Besides, he wasn't out *in* the woods, was he?"

That leavened Carrie's face somewhat, and the others at the table became more relaxed, as if they had feared something worse.

"Nah," Krystal said, rising, "he just went back to his cabin and ran into a killer. Didn't have to be him. Could have been anyone, like what happened to Sebastian."

Heads nodded. Then one man said, "Although I have to admit—Mason seemed the likeliest person someone would want to kill."

An uneasy laugh passed around the table.

"But not Sebastian," Carrie reminded them.

As they walked away from the table, Josh fell into step with Krystal. "Thoughts?"

"Nothing except that people seem to be finding their own relationship between Mason's storytelling and what happened. How unlikely is that?"

"Very. Unless Mason Cambridge was suicidal."

"Always a possibility, I suppose."

Just around then, soldiers returning from their escort duties began to come through the door. As was usual, given their training, they fell into step, a heavy tread.

"Packages delivered, sir," one former corporal said, stepping forward. "Just a few more to go."

"And nothing unusual?"

"Nothing we saw, unfortunately. Whoever was behind this has gone to ground."

Not good news, Josh thought. Looking at Krystal he saw his doubts reflected there. Nothing but a possible woman's boot print, which he well knew could mean anything or nothing. Men came in smaller sizes and weights, not just women.

He spoke to Krystal. "So Mason was popular with the ladies?"

"Flies to honey and all those aphorisms. Yeah, they hung on his every word."

Josh repressed a smile at Krystal's evident dislike of the writer. "Not one of his fans, huh?"

"Hardly. I kept telling Mom not to let him come, but he was a drawing card. The kind of headliner that was good for business."

"Didn't you agree?"

Krystal faced him, hands on her hips. "I could have tolerated him in smaller doses."

Then they resumed their walk around the room. Sunlight had begun to give way to the hints of another stormy day, and the remaining guests had begun to look uneasy again, as if they wanted to pull the curtains closed.

Except that made keeping an eye out for a threat almost impossible.

Gage had said he was shorthanded, looking for help. Josh eyed the troops who had come in to warm up and eat and decided to take a risk with their reaction.

He joined them, a roll in hand, coffee in the other. "I'm looking for some volunteers," he said quietly. "No one who's uncomfortable with the idea. Hell, that's why we built the stockade, so we wouldn't have to deal with this crap."

A half dozen nods answered him.

Josh drew a long breath, acutely aware of what he'd already asked of these vets. "I need some patrols out there. The sheriff is shorthanded."

He wasn't surprised by the hesitation. These people

had already left their safe zone to face hazards they knew all too well. Hazards they still had trouble dealing with.

Then one of them nodded. Rusty Rodes, a former MP. "I'll do it," he said. "There's something going on out there that needs to be stopped. I'll see who else will join me." Then he held up his mug with a half smile. "Heating up first, boss."

In the back office, opening the slatted blinds on the window that offered a view of the large lodge room, Krystal watched. Josh joined her and surprised Krystal by wrapping his arm around her. A secure feeling without a sense of encroachment. She had to fight an urge to rest her head against his powerful shoulder.

"What do you think?" he asked presently.

"That no one knows a damn thing about what's going on out there. Not a thing."

"Yeah. Some help."

Krystal sighed and scanned the room once more. "Another storm. I wonder if we'll get crowded again. We're not exactly stashed with enough provisions for days of this."

Josh understood the logistical problem. It was written into his genes after his war experiences. "Count on Gage Dalton."

"This entire county counts on that man. You'd think he'd have had enough of us by now."

"Is there often trouble up here?"

Krystal shook her head with a restrained laugh. "Usually we're pretty much boring. People just want to work."

"A different summer, then."

But, unable to help himself, Josh turned toward her. He didn't wind her in his arms much as he wanted to—that damn window blind was open.

He caught Krystal's gaze, drinking in her delicate features, even that small nose some people would have killed for, and smiled the warmest smile he still had in his heart.

"Lady," he said quietly, "I want to have sex with you right now. I want to strip you naked and fall into your depths and never emerge again."

He heard her sharp gasp of indrawn air, then she didn't breathe at all. Her face softened in every inch, but she said nothing.

He raised his hands and took her gently by her upper arms. "That's a promise," he said quietly. "You can kick it back in my teeth, but it's my promise to you."

"Oh, Josh," she murmured. "Oh, Josh. Please. But when this stuff is over."

He could have swept her into a tight embrace, to answer her need with his own, but that damn window...

Reluctantly he stepped back. "Soon."

"Not soon enough."

At that moment Joan chose to enter the office. She scanned the two of them as if she'd missed nothing at all, then nodded. "Wondered when" was all she said about them.

Krystal flushed faintly. "No news?"

Joan shook her head. "Nada. But there's something weird about that Mary Collins. Can't put my finger on it, though."

"The romance novelist?" Josh asked.

"The same. Never saw such a bitter woman in my life. At least she published a book." Joan sighed. "Of course, some folks will *never* be happy."

Josh stood looking out the window. "She's the one with the stringy dirty-blond hair, glasses, right? I swear she's been playing cards by herself this whole time."

His head tipped back a bit. "An interesting response to all of this, wouldn't you say?"

Krystal couldn't help but agree. "As if she feels she has nothing to fear."

"Yep. Except she was on *this* side of the glass when that bullet came flying through." He rubbed his face. "Hell, my kingdom for a decent clue."

"Well," Krystal said, "I'm all for talking to Mary right now. I'll tell her I need a touch of her zen." With a steady stride, she headed that way.

Josh decided to hang back, sitting with Donna Carstairs, who was eating a thin peanut butter sandwich. "Want one?" she asked, holding a half out toward him.

"I think I can smear my own peanut butter."

Donna chuckled. "Bread's getting stale, though. You'd best toast it."

"I've eaten bread so stale I could see where Fleming got his idea for penicillin."

Donna's laugh rose from her belly and Joan's laugh joined hers. Joan said, "I bet you and your group have quite some tales to tell, if they ever want to."

"Maybe so. Depends on how people around here feel about us."

Donna nodded and shoved half her sandwich his way. "A spread of opinions. Eat anyway. I'm sure you've heard them all. Some people want to think you're dangerous even though you've done nothing to scare them. Others figure it's none of their business. Then there are some who feel sympathy, at a safe distance. The whole gamut."

Josh nodded and turned his attention to Krystal. He couldn't tell if she was getting anything at all out of Mary.

"Now that one's interesting," Donna remarked. "Mary.

She comes nearly every year, and nearly every year she pretty much avoids Mason. Not that she's the only one."

Joan snorted. "Not everyone liked that literary lion. Comes on too strong for some. But to kill him?" Joan shrugged. "What would that gain?"

Josh had an idea. "A lot of money for his agent and publisher. Nothing like a dead writer."

Joan nodded slowly. "Won't say that hasn't come up before, but I'd remove that agent, Darlene, from the list. If that woman ever stops shaking it'll be in her next life-time."

Then Josh spoke heavily. "Or maybe she didn't know how awful it could be to kill another human."

Joan's gaze met his directly. "So tell me, Josh. Is it awful?"

Josh closed his eyes, stomping down on a flood of memories he needed to control, resisting his urge to yell at Joan for even daring to ask such a question. "Yeah," he said finally. "It's that god-awful."

Joan at least didn't offer any fake sympathy. "I figured" was all she said.

"It's better that way. To feel that way."

"Maybe. Maybe we wouldn't go to war as often."

Joan sighed and turned to Donna, whose face had tightened. "How much can we feed this small mob?"

Donna jerked her chin toward the darkening day. "It'll be pretty thin unless Gage shows up with the supplies he promised."

Joan snorted. "Like he doesn't have a thousand other people to take care of right now."

Donna answered quietly. "Like he doesn't have a couple of murders to take care of right now." Then she looked pleadingly at Joan and Josh. "What the hell happened here? This isn't our kind of place, not anymore."

Josh leaned forward, claiming Donna's attention. "It'll be okay when we get this done. Something crazy happened, but it won't happen forever."

He wished he believed that. None of this was adding up to any kind of sense. Murdered SOB author? Possible. Even likely. But that poet guy, so inoffensive he faded into the background? Paul had been pretty clear about that.

He was relieved when Krystal finally ended her conversation with Mary Collins. Maybe she'd gotten some useful information.

Krystal paused to speak to a few people who were ensconced at their own tables. Outside, the storm began to blow again, though not as wildly as yesterday.

At last she reached the office, grabbed a cup of coffee and sat with the others.

"Well?" Joan demanded.

"Mary absolutely didn't have the highest opinion of Mason Cambridge, I can tell you that for sure."

Josh leaned forward. "As in?"

"As in she thought he was a disgusting creep not above stealing the works of others."

Josh leaned back immediately. He hadn't expected such a bold accusation. "Stealing?"

Krystal merely shook her head. "The woman doesn't get the difference between copyright infringement and copyright in general. She's not the only one on the planet."

"How so?"

Krystal accepted a roll from Donna. "How long will these rolls last?" she asked Donna.

"Let's just say I'm about to remember how to bake again. You can help."

Krystal smiled and nodded. "I remember those lessons when I was a kid. Messy."

"You can't make fresh dough without being messy."

Josh had reached the point of tapping his fingers impatiently on the tabletop. "Mary?" he prompted.

Krystal bit into her roll and wiped her mouth. "Nothing in particular except I don't think she'd have trusted Mason further than she could throw him."

"Why not?"

Krystal dropped her roll half-eaten. "A lot of writers, and not just Mary, from what I gather, believe there's a copyright on ideas. You come up with a brilliant idea and it's yours. Nobody can take it. Except that's not true. Take Star Wars, for example. Anybody can use that term, but it's the graphic way it's presented that's copyrighted and trademarked. Regardless, no idea is copyrighted, and to prove that one is actually stolen would be a hell of a legal task. Hell, a writer can't even copyright her own name."

"So there are a lot of people running around with the wrong idea?"

"A lot who don't seem to understand just how limited copyright protection is. Regardless, Mary isn't the only one, from what she said."

"Well, that lengthens the list," Josh remarked, looking out across the room, a room that was slowly becoming more occupied.

"I guess that depends on who you think would murder over it." Krystal pushed her cup and roll aside. "I don't like Mary."

Joan stiffened. "Why not? She's never been a problem in the past."

"I don't know." Krystal shifted her attention to Josh. "You know what I mean, I bet. Something in the eyes."

He knew all too well exactly what she meant. "Hell" was his only answer.

"What should we do?" Donna asked.

"Keep an eye out," Josh replied. "And I'm going to ask the same of some more of my troops. I just need to know how many we need to watch."

Krystal reached impulsively across the table, understanding now some of what Josh dealt with. "Would that be good for them?"

"Their choice," Josh said evenly. "Nobody gets forced. Maybe for some it will even be good." Hadn't he caught a glimpse of that earlier? Glad to be on task again? Glad to have a purpose. Maybe it would be the best thing in the end for some of them.

He rose. "I'm going to go talk to some more of my soldiers. See what kind of response I get."

Krystal rose, too. "Can I come?"

Josh scanned her. "For what purpose?"

"Maybe a woman would give all this more purpose."

What the hell did she mean by that? Josh scowled but didn't prevent her. As if Carly Narth, a woman, didn't already do that with her scars. Or maybe Carly just seemed too tough.

Mentally shrugging, he led the way to the door, to where a few of his people waited. Then out the door and onto the porch. The wind blew, but not as stiffly as yesterday. The rain even seemed gentler.

And they waited, six of them, milling around, looking for orders.

As soon as Josh appeared, they gave him their full attention. They hardly seemed to see Krystal.

"I'm looking," Josh said, "for some who are willing to stand guard, keep an eye out. Something is going on out there, although at this point I can't be sure it isn't inside."

He noted that Carly Narth stepped closer to Krystal, whether in a protective posture or in recognition of a kindred spirit, he couldn't tell. Regardless, as tough as he believed Krystal was, he had to feel better about Carly's experience. At least Krystal didn't seem to notice the gesture.

Soon he had even more of his soldiers ready to move out on a quiet mission. Garbed in the mountain camo clothing, they wouldn't stand out at all, and experience had taught them how to be stealthy.

Camo ponchos were gone, though, getting rid of any possible rustle of that fabric. Experience. Troops as prepared as they needed to be for the cold and wet. Admirable people. With a rough plan of action, they were ready.

He watched them filter into the woods singly, nearly invisible unless he had known what to look for. Only Carly remained and she looked at Krystal. "Ditch the yellow poncho. It's a target. You got any camo?"

"Some. From back when I used to hunt."

"Then get it on now. Don't need you sticking out like a sore thumb."

Krystal offered no objection, apparently recognizing the sense of the order. Stubborn as she could be at times, she showed none of it now.

Ten minutes later she returned in old-fashioned camo,

none of the modern infrared reflective gear. It would none-theless serve its purpose. He doubted the killer in the woods was supplied with the right kind of goggles. Too freaking expensive.

At least he hoped he wasn't wrong. He knew he and his soldiers had a few of the temperature-sensitive goggles between them, hardly a big supply but enough.

Hell. A killer or two on the loose in woods which pro-vided major protection for him or them just by itself. Or one or two hidden inside the lodge, where matters could get ugly in an eyeblink.

He looked at Reject, who had followed him to the open door. "Stand guard," he said, hoping the dog understood that much.

He could have sworn the husky did, standing up taller on his damaged hind legs. Dogs and pain. He wished hu-mans could tolerate it as well.

Josh hated being on duty inside, but then he had a thought, a thought that should have occurred to him sooner: *he* was the psychologist. He was constantly eval-uating his own troops for their mental stability, but maybe he should be observing the people in the lodge much more closely. Hell.

Then out of the misty day emerged Harris Belcher, the owner of the sled dog teams. He headed straight for Josh. "Want any K-9 help?"

Josh started to shake his head. "You can't risk your dogs, Harris. Expensive, well-trained…"

"I wasn't thinking about risking them all. I can take a team out the way I did looking for Reject. And trust me, they all remember that odor of the bastard who hurt Re-ject and they don't like it."

"But the killer might have moved on, might be seeking targets from a different location."

Harris shook his blond head. "Won't make any difference. These dogs are able to smell weak ice. They won't have forgotten this odor. Damn near as good as bloodhounds."

Josh hated the idea. His troops had a choice whether to take these risks, but the dogs didn't. On the other hand, they'd be useful, very useful.

"Just don't risk too many," he said at last.

Harris gave him a crooked smile. "You ever seen how fast these dogs can escape danger?"

"I hope I don't have to."

But then he watched the dogs head for the woods. Might as well have been wearing white targets on their tails, although not all of them. Some had fairly dark coloration. Regardless, after a whistle from Harris, the pack seemed to get the order to spread out. No pulling in a team this time.

Carly and Krystal weren't far behind. He hated not being able to follow them, but he needed to keep an eye on the interior of the lodge. No idea in the world where these threats had come from, not if the killers could have moved inside with the group of clients.

Still, he would have preferred to be out there with Carly, doing something more useful. Except that he knew Carly well enough by now to realize how she would take offense at that. After what she had been through, she wasn't about to allow anyone to suggest she wasn't capable in even the smallest way.

So two women he cared about marched into the treacherous forest and he was forced to stay behind. That didn't suit his personality at all. He especially hated to see Krystal marching into that dangerous darkness.

The protector in him was emerging full-time and his fists kept clenching and unclenching. God, he hated having his hands tied like this.

And scanning the room for someone acting odd seemed like hardly a great use of his time.

KRYSTAL WAS GLAD to be moving through the forest with Carly. No telling how much they'd accomplish, given the acreage out here, but it was better than nothing. She suspected Josh wasn't feeling any better.

"Josh doesn't like being stuck like this," Krystal murmured.

"No. Shh."

Carly was right, of course. This was no time for gab that might give them away. The deeper they sank into the dimly lit forest, the further they seemed to slip into danger. At one point Carly held up her finger, freezing them both in place, listening intently.

Then a husky raced by, tail fully raised and fluffed. Carly pointed and the two of them did their best to follow the dog. It wasn't easy.

The dog leaped easily over obstacles that tried to trip the two women. It soon left them behind and Carly and Krystal stopped and looked at each other, panting.

"I'd like to know what he smelled," Carly whispered.

Krystal nodded.

Just then, a loud crack, only slightly smothered by the wet trees, tore the air wide open.

The two women exchanged looks, then started hurrying back toward the lodge, keeping low.

A gunshot. Almost impossible to tell where it came from, but they worried about the people in the lodge.

THE BULLET CAME through the window from the outside. A second shot rent the air. Reject sent up a howl fit to raise the dead. The lodge's clients hit the floor as fast as Olympic divers.

Josh swore, lowered himself to a deep knee bend and inched toward the window. From outside. That meant the killer was still out there. Now to hunt him while keeping the people indoors safe.

As soon as he could, he pulled his walkie off his belt and raised his team.

One didn't answer. "Rodes," he said again, his voice sharp.

"Got him" came the voice of Angus. "Hit through the thigh."

"Bad?"

"Not an artery. Cleary and Janice are moving in to help carry him."

Josh felt as if a bomb were about to explode inside him. Rusty, of all people. A former MP with a spine of hardened steel. A steady personality despite his demons.

But Josh had another, more immediate concern. He looked around at all the civilians crouched on the floor, lying face down. Terrified, as well they should be.

"I'm going outside. Joan, you still got that shotgun?"

"Believe it. Nobody's getting in here."

Donna edged toward Josh. "You can't go out there alone. Don't be a damn fool."

With a murderer out there? No, he wasn't a damn fool, but he didn't want anyone else to be one either. Everything about Donna said that there was no way possible to keep her inside short of tying her up. She even carried a chef's knife, for the love of Pete.

Joan spoke quietly. "Donna," she said warningly.

Donna answered just as quietly, "You do your job in here. Joan, there's a killer out there. Protect these people."

Josh eyed Donna. "Why should I make an exception for you?"

"Two years of infantry training before I busted a knee. I'm good enough."

Joan fell silent.

Protecting these people was what it was all about. Josh crept toward the door as Reject let out another bone-chilling howl.

Why, he wondered, had nature given huskies the same howl as wolves. Because it sure made the blood want to curdle.

ALSO LYING ON the floor was a woman scared out of her wits and wondering what the hell had happened to her careful plan to get rid of one lousy writer. Just Mason Cambridge. Had she asked so much?

The guy was a bald thief without the least bit of shame or compunction. He deserved to die. Maybe Sebastian had been a brilliant diversion.

Or not. Because a second bullet had come through that window and she became convinced this time it was directed at *her*.

Because only *she* could identify the perp. The guy with the trigger finger. The guy who had stabbed Sebastian.

God, the thought of a stabbing made her sick to her

stomach. One gunshot, neat and clean, should have been enough. But not for this jackass.

She'd had nothing against Sebastian, anyway. He'd always been respectful. Unlike one man who thought he was God's gift to the literary world.

Not even Mary thought her writing reached that level, of being God's gift. She wrote to entertain. She wrote to distract people from the realities of life. To give them a break.

And Mason had stolen all of that for his own, then acted as if *he* mattered. As if he were the only one who mattered.

Now here she was, lying on a floor, scared out of her mind and wondering if her coconspirator was coming to protect himself by killing her before she could talk.

As if she'd ever admit anything. But he didn't know that.

Then another bullet cracked the glass, this time leaving a crazed web of cracks all over it.

The shots were getting closer. She looked around, wondering if she could find a better place to hide.

CARLY AND KRYSTAL heard the next two gunshots, seeming louder this time despite the dripping leaves. Carly leaned close to Krystal's ear. "We need to circle in around the sound."

Krystal nodded, understanding. Assuming one shooter, their only chance of catching him was encirclement.

If there were two shooters, they were out of luck, but better to take down one than none.

Krystal was also developing the sickening feeling that this shooter had a target in mind inside the lodge. Why else would he be shooting from the outside? But who could that target be?

Mason made sense. Sebastian hadn't, of course, but who knew that man very well? But to go after someone else in that building? More secrets? More ugliness? Did any of them really know each other that well, despite some of the artists having visited for years?

Hell, no. Mason had, as far as she knew, been the only resident to run around advertising himself, his success and his abrasive personality. But who could know what might have been running beneath among the quieter of the others?

God, she thought as she and Carly crept through the wet woods, separating slowly from one another as they tried to localize as best they could where they'd heard the shots come from.

Krystal wasn't at all used to this kind of searching and hunting. Never had she felt her civilian inexperience as much as she did then. She got the principle, but she didn't have the practice. Keeping low to the ground, belly-crawling a couple of times, she could only hope she was doing this correctly.

And noticing, for the very first time, that a forest floor that had always seemed smooth enough when she walked over it now held a million little tortures in the form of sharp broken branches and twigs. At least that helped focus her on something besides crawling toward death.

Chapter Eleven

Josh surveyed the indoor scene, the people glued to the floor. He prayed that one of them didn't panic enough to stand. So far, none had.

And Joan looked quite businesslike with her shotgun. Anybody who tried to get in might not live to talk about it. Donna had at least subsided, taking an order to keep an eye on Joan.

But there was a shooter outside. One, as far as he could tell. The sound seemed mostly centered, although it was moving around a bit. It had to have been to get Rusty.

Reject let out another low growl, hunched on the floor but appearing ready to spring.

The dog recognized the size of the threat out there.

Josh made a signal to Joan, who nodded from her guard-post near the kitchen.

With everyone on the floor, Josh felt he needed to get outside and try to locate the shooter. God, wildly pumping bullets into a room like this was madness. Anyone could have been wounded or killed. How could there possibly be a target among all these people?

He looked around the room at frightened faces, at bodies plastered to the floor, and began to signal with his hand for everyone to remain low. All he needed at this point was for someone to lose their head and leap upward in an attempt to flee. And there was simply no way to prevent it.

He kept low, to be invisible from the windows, hating the way it slowed him down. He hoped the rest took the hint.

But Josh had to try to locate the shooter. He needed to be proactive, not simply wait here for the next step in the shooter's plan—if he even had one.

Josh signaled once more for everyone to remain low, away from the line of sight from the windows. Out of harm's way insomuch as possible.

Then he opened one of the two front doors as quietly as he could, given that the rain had made hinges want to squeal. This time nature favored him. Not all the lubricant had failed.

Slipping out that door seemed almost too easy to do. The day's attempt at sunshine had already failed. Then to his utter annoyance, his sat phone beeped once.

Hell, he should have silenced it. But anything coming over it was likely to be important.

It was Angus. "Can't send you any more help. Mudslide downslope, sheriff and every spare hand are digging people out."

"Copy," Josh answered quietly, then put the phone on a quiet vibrate, kicking himself for not having done it sooner.

He waited for any sign that the call had been heard, but no sound came back at him. Maybe the shooter wasn't listening for anything so minor. Maybe he was more absorbed in his beastly task.

Regardless, Josh's heart squeezed until he felt the breath was being stolen from him. Krystal was out there.

Carly had plenty of experience and would look after her, but not every possibility could be accounted for.

He might lose Krystal before he even got the chance to really know her.

Of all the losses he'd faced in his life, that one loomed as being among the largest.

KRYSTAL WASN'T DOING much better emotionally as she crept along the forest floor. She was terrified for all the people inside the lodge but she was even more terrified for Josh.

It seemed wrong, somehow, to value one person over another, but her heart wasn't listening anyway.

Josh had come unexpectedly, unwantedly, into her life, and she wasn't ready to let him go. Even if he wanted to go back to hiding in his stockade with his soldiers she doubted she would let him.

Not that he'd been hiding, she reminded herself. But he'd closed himself off so completely from the outside world that she could scarcely believe how quickly he'd melded himself into her life.

In just a few days, Josh Healey had emerged from privacy into the wider world of Cash Creek Canyon and had become respected by many. Maybe even liked. Her mother sure liked him.

She eased farther along the wet ground, ignoring a sharp stick that poked her thigh. She knew she was distracting herself with thoughts of Josh. Those could come later.

Right now there were a whole lot of people who needed protecting.

At least the shooter seemed to be focused on the lodge

rather than individual cabins. Whether that might change was enough to make her heart jam into her throat.

All this open space. All these residents essentially unprotected by anyone. Even Josh's soldiers and the deputies creeping around out here couldn't possibly create a tight enough noose to prevent a single shooter from getting through.

Faintly she heard Carly moving through her part of the pincer movement. At least that's what Krystal thought it was called. She began to wonder if the retreat's "no guns" rule had been a wise one after all.

Except, she thought in a moment of irrepressible humor, imagine all these artists taking potshots from their cabins because something frightened them. This place would become a shooting gallery. If it wasn't already.

JOSH EASED ALONG the porch of the lodge, then down onto the wet ground. Twice now the shooter had chosen to blast holes in the windows and once had hit Rusty. What other area might he choose?

It would sure as hell help to know what the guy was after. What he was hoping to accomplish. Fish in a bowl was hardly a guide.

Could the guy just be interested in killing? He wouldn't be the first. Josh had seen those broken minds before. Minds that had crossed some internal barrier between respect for life and total disregard for it. Some even became excited by it. Justified by it.

He was also sure it wouldn't be long before fingers started to be pointed at his soldiers, albeit wrongly.

People wanted to believe vets with PTSD were dangerously violent, even when most of them only suffered from pain and misery and an attempt to block it from their own heads. Many were better off left in solitude or the company of others who shared their experience. Almost none wanted to hurt anyone else. They hurt enough within themselves.

He slipped farther along into the semidarkness of the still-dripping woods, listening for any betraying sound. Maybe this guy had discovered his own true nature when he killed Mason Cambridge.

Because something about the wildness of this attack seemed to have come from nowhere. Whoever the shooter was, it was highly unlikely he'd ever done this before. Nothing about this seemed carefully planned, merely carried out.

So what here had brought this all about?

Mason Cambridge? The epicenter of a lot of hate and anger. The man more than one person had pointed to as likely to be hated enough to be a victim.

But that wouldn't explain Sebastian, unless he was meant to be a diversion. Then there were these random gunshots through the windows. There had to be a point.

Surely this creep must have a point in all this, however nonsensical. Surely he must realize he was making a bigger target of *himself*. That far more people would be hunting for him now.

So what might make him not care? Or did he think all of this confusion would protect him? Protect him from what?

Josh's mind was running overtime, trying to build some kind of profile that would help him hunt this killer.

And running overtime worrying about Krystal.

KRYSTAL FROZE AS another sharp crack tore through the air. Then, after a terrible moment, it was followed by a scream. Maybe two of them. Oh, God, had someone been shot?

She began to crawl more quickly through the undergrowth, heedless now of all the poking and hot ripping of her skin. This had to be stopped at any cost.

JOSH HEARD THE fourth shot as he was edging his way into the thicker woods. He still had a view of the lodge windows through the tree branches, though it was broken now by the greenery, the glass crazed by the earlier shot.

It was still enough. The scream caused his heart to freeze for just an instant. He knew that sound: someone else had been shot. He could only wonder how this might be affecting his people, who had had enough of those sounds to haunt their lives forever.

God! Trying to hurry his steps toward the last sound of the rifle without giving himself away slowed him down, made him feel like a charging bull who could race through any obstacle to reach the shooter except that he was continuously blocked.

Except the shooter could escape in these dense woods. Josh pulled his KA-BAR off his belt, ready. No crawling, not now. Only crouching as necessary.

Out there were his own soldiers, those who could face this threat. Closing in, he was sure. These people knew how to tell where a gunshot sprang from. As long as the sound didn't reawaken horrors that had driven them to these woods.

But Krystal was out there, too, knowing nothing about how to handle such a situation.

God, he was torn between getting that damn shooter

and racing out to help Krystal. Although Carly must be keeping her safe. Must have made it clear how to move surreptitiously.

He paused, fist clenched around his knife, and listened.

The falling of remaining raindrops from the trees didn't help at all, but faintly, just faintly, he believed he heard someone sliding over the ground, judging it had to be one of his soldiers. Few civilians knew how to be that quiet.

Approaching as quietly as possible. With any luck, the shooter wouldn't recognize the sound.

Nor should he, given his rampage. He was out for one thing only, and it didn't involve worrying about quiet sounds in the woods. In fact, Josh would guess at this point that the guy didn't care at all if he got caught.

A vendetta. But against whom? Who the hell had triggered this guy into this shooting spree?

Josh couldn't even imagine what might be the trigger, although given his psychological training he ought to be getting a clearer picture by now.

But all of that seemed to be escaping because of his determination, his concern about Krystal and the other guests.

And damn it all to hell, Krystal was out there unarmed except for a chef's knife he thought he'd seen her carry out. But how could she know what to do with it? Unlike Carly, unlike himself and others in their group, Krystal had no knife training.

He could have cursed a blue streak, but that all had to remain silently locked in his mind, where it offered no release at all.

Moving closer to where he had heard the last shot, he

hoped he would get there before anyone else did. He'd gladly lay down his life before anyone else got hurt.

He'd lay it down for Krystal in a heartbeat.

Then there had been the scream from within the lodge. Someone had been wounded. God willing, someone in that place knew how to provide decent first aid.

He sped up his steps as much as he dared. Maybe it was time to draw the killer's attention. Right at himself. Away from everyone else.

KRYSTAL FORGOT EVERYTHING else when she heard the scream from the lodge. Her mother. All their friends. If that SOB had hurt or killed someone…

Forgetting everything Carly had been trying to teach her, Krystal shoved herself up from the wet ground and began to run toward the lodge. To hell with caution and catching the guy. That could come later. Right now someone had screamed from within those supposedly safe walls.

Someone might be dying while tree roots hampered her every step.

SHE REACHED THE front door at last and burst into the lodge, ready for almost anything. Or so she thought.

What she was not prepared for was the sight of Mel Marbly, their longtime handyman, holding the entire room captive at the point of a rifle.

"Get in here," Mel growled. "But before you do," he shouted, "you tell those jackasses out there that if one of them comes through that door now I'm going to shoot your mother."

Krystal's legs weakened, but she had no doubt Mel

could do as he threatened. Her mother lay in plain sight on the floor.

As did so many others who could be killed.

Having no choice, her hands shaking, she opened the front door and called out, hoping everyone heard her.

Then she heard a distant walkie crackle, followed by another. The word was being passed. Thank God. Reassurance that the situation was known helped her even though she knew it might do no good. At least she wasn't facing this alone.

Then she looked at the threat, trying to figure out if there was anything at all she could do. Especially since Mel held the deadlier weapon.

"Drop that knife," he said. "Now. Kick it away."

She dropped the chef's knife, certain it had been practically useless in her hands anyway. She kicked it aside, then faced Mel, hoping to take his attention from everyone else.

"Why are you doing this, Mel?"

The man sneered, actually sneered. In all the time Krystal had known him, she was sure she had not seen that expression on his face.

"Mel? Did something happen? Did something make you really angry?"

Mel snorted. "Like you didn't all see it. Like any of you did a damn thing about it. Except one of you. One of you hated him enough to take action."

Her chest tightening, Krystal scanned the floor, wondering what collaborator Mel might be hiding here. Someone who might be as much of a threat? *God!* Then Mel snapped her back to the moment.

"Big-deal author," Mel growled. "Except he didn't have a new thought of his own during his entire career. He stole ideas like cherries to be plucked off a tree. He even stole some from that famous writer, what's his name? It's a wonder other writers didn't sue the pants off him."

Krystal's nerves tightened as she watched the way the gun barrel jerked around, as if Mel couldn't focus on a single victim.

"Why didn't any of you sue him?" Mel demanded of his hostages.

Nobody seemed to want to answer, understandably, given the way things were. Raising a voice might be the last thing anyone did.

So Krystal took it on herself, not caring if she sounded irritated with Mel. Caring only that she grabbed his attention.

"Sheesh, Mel, do you have any idea how expensive it is to sue for copyright infringement? How long it takes? And how freaking hard it is to prove?"

"If you steal…"

Krystal was already well tired of this argument. "For God's sake, Mel, how do you prove something was stolen? Seriously. *Your* idea? Shakespeare probably already had it. Your words? How many of them will it take before a judge will decide it's no accident? Then there's you, the writer. You make that kind of trouble, chances are no publisher will want to touch you with a ten-foot pole. So you kill your own career."

Mel's hand wavered, but only a bit. He was staring at someone, but Krystal couldn't tell whom.

"How would *you* know?" he demanded.

"Because every so often someone is an idiot enough to try to sue a big-name author. And if you follow the story you see the same thing. It can't be proven for a lot of reasons. Oh, once in a while someone succeeds, but not often."

Mel glared at her and Krystal didn't like the look in his eyes. Death seemed to be written there and she feared for everyone in the room.

Where were Josh and his people? Too far away in the woods to be of much help? Yet she was counting on him with her whole heart even though she knew she had to find a way to act herself. Who knew how far away he might be, and all these people depended on her.

Trying to think of another distraction, she spoke again. "Mel? Can I sit down? I hurt my leg out there."

He gave a short laugh, as if he didn't care, then waved the gun barrel toward an empty chair. Far enough from others that she couldn't protect anyone. Not what she wanted, but her only choice.

"Thank you," she said, feigning a gratitude she didn't at all feel. A quick scan told her the chef's knife was still too far away. God, she needed this man to make a mistake. An important one.

Mel continued to wave the gun around, a danger to everyone if his finger slipped on that trigger. It might, Krystal thought, gripping the seat of her chair with her hands until they felt white-knuckled. How could she prevent that, especially when Mel appeared to have started sweating.

"You feeling okay, Mel?"

He scowled. "That ain't gonna work on me. I'm just fine and you quit saying I might not be. I could decide to shoot *you*."

Krystal drew a long, shaky breath and put her life on the line. "Then why don't you, Mel? Just kill me now."

Joan made a whimper from where she lay near the kitchen, but Mel didn't glance her way. "Your mom could be next."

Krystal bit her lip. "Is something special about me, Mel? Why you don't want to shoot me this very minute?"

He shook his head, but the gun in his hands shook with the movement, just slightly. "Ain't got no problem with you, ladybug. You've always been nice to me. Nice to every damn person in here, even them that don't deserve it. Nah. I'd rather kill your ma. She's the one who keeps bringing that Mason back every damn year."

Krystal caught her breath. It was true. She saw her mother's eyes, saw the terror in them. *Do something*, Krystal told herself. *Do something before this guy gets out of hand.*

Mel raised the barrel of his gun just a bit. "Six shots in here, ladybug. Six. Then I got a clip with another ten. That's a lot of these idiots I can get rid of."

"But why should you want to?"

"Because that man treated me like crap! Every time he saw me. You think I give a real damn that he stole other people's work? Everyone complained about it, but not one of these cowards tried to do a damn thing about it. Not one. Bunch of scaredy-cats, sucking up to a man they think is a thief. Or maybe he wasn't so much the bad guy. I only know of one book he stole."

Quiet settled over the room.

"Whose?" Krystal demanded. "Whose book?"

Mel shook his head. "Why should I tell you if she won't?"

That was when Krystal began to scan the faces on the

floor. A woman. Maybe that woman with the strangely dead eyes. Except those eyes looked terrified now, not dead.

What the hell was going on here?

OUTSIDE, JOSH WAS wondering pretty much the same thing. His soldiers were steadily gathering, along with deputies who'd been left behind to help. Gathering, ready for a large attack if one seemed warranted. But those damn windows might as well be opaque. No heads could be seen except that of one man, waving a rifle. A rifle that could get off six shots in quick order, more if he had a clip. A lot of people injured or dead.

More curses filled his head. Angus reached his side.

"Not looking good, boss," Angus muttered.

"Yeah. Civilians."

"Civilians were always the problem."

Too true. There were a lot of lives in there that had to be protected without setting off that creep with his dangerous rifle.

Josh closed his eyes briefly, trying to draw a mental image of the situation inside, trying hard not to picture Krystal in the middle of it. One person, no matter how loved, could inadvertently cause a distraction that led to chaos. Given his growing feelings for that one brave, lovely woman, she could cause that distraction.

Reaching deep within himself, Josh sought the detachment that had carried him through so many dangerous, deadly times. A detachment that could make decisions without overweighing the consequences.

People mattered, individuals mattered. But then there was the mission.

BESIDE HIM, Angus stirred. He had his radio set to as low a volume as he could get. Josh barely heard the murmuring between the troops.

"Soon," Angus said to him. "Everyone's pulling together in a tight cordon."

"Then what?" Josh asked almost sharply. "Yeah, we can storm the place but what about all those people in there? Hell, Angus, you don't need me to draw a map."

"Nah," Angus muttered. "I wish you could, Colonel."

So did Josh. He stared at those messed-up windows. Too bad he couldn't see more from here. Which left only one choice, a choice that might cause harm all by itself. If his soldiers became protective of him. If he got noticed by the bad guy inside. A dangerous choice but none were left.

"Angus, let everyone know I'm going on a solo recon. Don't anybody move. We gotta have some idea what's going on in there. Damn, we don't even know how many armed people are holding those hostages or who might be where."

"No kidding. Keep low, boss."

A reminder so obvious it could only be said out of caring. He gave Angus a friendly punch to his upper arm, then began creeping through restarting rain.

Damn, when had this forest floor become so full of tree roots?

Distracting question and he knew it. He'd had plenty of experience with using distractions to distance himself from the deadly trouble approaching. Distractions, but not any that would reduce his focus.

Focus was the one thing he couldn't afford to sacrifice now. Krystal. He clenched his teeth until they ached. She was his focus, though not his only goal.

The leaves and pine needles beneath his feet felt nearly greasy with the rain. Only his tactical boots kept him from sliding.

For the first time since this mess had begun, he found himself wishing for a rifle. It would have given him more control at a greater distance.

Unfortunately it might also set off the gunman or gunmen inside. A spray of bullets out of their semiautomatic rifles could be fast and deadly. Too fast to counter until the damage had been done.

Swearing under his breath, he crept forward toward the windows, his only hope of getting a decent view of the inside. At least most of the curtains were still open because the morning—had it only been *this* morning?—had seemed so bright and cheerful.

Now the gray pall of the rain had settled in again, killing useful light, washing everything in depth-defying shadows.

Damn weather.

Finally he reached the porch. Now he had to move even more silently. Old wood creaked. Someone paying attention inside might hear it.

At least he heard no loud sobbing from inside the building. If someone had been shot, it hadn't been bad. Or maybe they were dead. The urge to kill was growing in him.

Creeping along the porch also filled him with a familiar anxiety. The kind that made him more cautious, that eased away any unnecessary fear.

Because there were some things he had ceased to fear at all, including his own death.

KRYSTAL'S MIND RAN at top speed as she sought to find an additional way to distract Mel. The man seemed to be enjoying waving that rifle entirely too much, as if he were looking forward to using it again.

Against the wall sat Julia Jansen, her leg grazed at the calf muscle, a tight bandage around it. Julia had grown pale, but she didn't appear to be losing a lot of blood. That was good.

But what had made Mel choose her for his first blast of death? Anything in particular?

"Mel," she said, drawing the man's attention her way again.

"Yeah. Why can't you just shut your damn mouth? You're gonna get one of these people shot."

She drew a long breath and closed her eyes. No, she couldn't leave Mel undistracted while he held that unsteady rifle.

"I get," she said quietly, opening her eyes, "why you hated Mason. But whatever did Sebastian do to you? He was so quiet and inoffensive."

"That's what *you* thought," Mel growled, waving the barrel around again as if it were nothing but a firecracker. "The guy pissed me off. Always creeping around. Always being nice to Mason. Weak, that's what he was. A suck-up."

Krystal nodded, not sure she was understanding this part at all, but what did it matter as long as Mel thought she did. With great effort, she didn't look at the windows although she was hoping to see half an army swing through them, guns blazing.

Except for everyone on the floor. Josh had to be thinking of them, too.

But as she listened to Mel, a conviction steadily grew inside her: Mel had not acted alone. He'd been provoked.

Urged. In some ways Mel was a weakling himself, as she'd seen from time to time over the years.

Someone *could* push him. He might even get creative on his own, but the original driving force? Not Mel.

Desperately she looked around at the faces hiding beneath tables and chairs. Did one of them hide a truly ugly secret? Would it help if she could get Mel to spill the identity or just make it worse?

God, she wished she had some kind of experience to measure this against.

Then her gaze settled on Mary Collins. She remembered all the hard-eyed looks Mary used to send Mason's way, but right now Mary appeared as terrified as any of them.

But why wouldn't she, even if she had started this? She might be the one who had unleashed the monster. But she certainly had every reason to be terrified of Mel now.

God, Josh, where are you?

JOSH WAS STILL creeping along the windows, peering through the cracked glass to build the necessary map in his head. Damn, there were so many people in there, people who needed protection. But so far he'd seen only one shooter, one guy waving his gun like he didn't know what it was good for. Waving it too close to Krystal.

Muttering another curse, he turned away from the windows and covered his mouth, speaking quietly into his sat phone. At least it didn't crackle like the walkies.

He laid out what he could see as best he could see it, focusing on the shooter. Making sure everyone understood that Krystal was sitting alone in front of the door.

From what little he could hear inside, he could tell she was doing her best to keep the shooter distracted.

Brilliant, tough woman. Admirable.

But now he had to work his way around to the front door and try to line up the troops in the safest way possible.

KRYSTAL WAS REACHING the end of patience and, along with it, fear. Oh, she feared for everyone in this room but was losing fear for herself. Each time she glanced at her mother, the ache was piercing. Somehow she had to protect Joan no matter what it cost.

Taking a stab in the dark, she looked directly at Mary Collins, speaking directly to her. "Why'd you have Mel kill Sebastian? What did that man ever do to you?"

"I didn't make anyone kill him," Mary said, her voice leavening with fear.

"Nah," Mel agreed. "Except she thought it was a good idea after. 'Cuz then it wouldn't make any kind of sense about Mason. She liked my idea good enough then."

At that, Mary stood up, hardly seeing all the people scattered around her. "I never should have trusted you." Her voice quaked but her eyes had grown hard again.

"Maybe not," Mel said, waving the gun her way. "But I was smarter than you. All these folks running around wondering why these two guys should get killed. Didn't make no sense nohow. Puzzle piece that don't fit. Remember I told you about them? You thought I was smart then. Smarter than you because you never figured it out yourself."

Mary kept her hands still, as if she knew she faced serious danger from Mel. Krystal tried to judge if she could move fast enough—would she be able to wrestle that rifle from Mel's hands? Before he killed half the people in this room?

She readied her muscles, but even as she did so she realized she didn't have the leverage to leap that far.

"Guess you were going to get away," Mel said. "Leave me behind to face it all. Bet you didn't think I figured that out, did you?"

Now Mary was looking fearful again. "We had an agreement."

"Didn't have an agreement that you'd skip out and leave me behind."

"Damn it," Mary said, bursting out from her fear. "You were supposed to leave, too. And if you hadn't killed Sebastian…"

"If I hadn't killed Sebastian, what? You coulda sued Mason for years, but you spent your time just hating him. Nursing a need for vengeance. You got your vengeance, lady. And maybe you're the one I should be leaving behind."

Mel raised his rifle, pointing straight at Mary.

Then, after being silent all this time, Reject let out the most frightening howl, long, almost endless. Krystal's skin tingled as Mel became startled enough to aim his rifle at the dog.

But Reject had already leaped, flying toward Mary as if he had picked out a threat. Just as Krystal felt this was her only chance to take a leap at Mel, the doors behind her burst open with a loud bang. Glass from the windows finished shattering all over the floor.

Josh and his soldiers had arrived and in no time at all had Mel zip-tied. Mary tried to run but Krystal was having none of it. Changing her trajectory, she headed straight for the woman who had started all of this.

And Reject stormed along right beside her.

Chapter Twelve

After the hellish hours that had just passed, Krystal felt as if time sped up to almost overwhelming speed.

Mary Collins had managed to scratch Krystal's cheek, which the paramedics insisted on treating even though Krystal thought it was superficial.

She spent a long time hugging her mother, the two of them alternately crying and laughing with relief. They stood beside stretchers as Julia and Rusty were carried out by paramedics. They watched as Mary and Mel were carted out in handcuffs by Gage Dalton and his deputies. As it should be.

But she could scarcely believe the anger and rage that Mary screamed as she was carried away. All these years Mary had hidden those feelings so well that all Krystal had recognized of her before was that she had ice in her eyes when she saw Mason. Hardly a surprising thing, given Mason.

Still, it was shocking to see what had been right under her nose, a threat almost beyond imagination. And the saddest thing of all was that Sebastian had paid the price of his life merely to provide a distraction.

The minds of some people would always be beyond her grasp. Always.

THE LODGE BEGAN to quiet down. Voices that had been filled with disbelief and excitement gave way to a deeper silence as events began to sink in. They'd been held hostage at gunpoint.

Two among them had been killers.

Krystal thought she saw distrust in some of the faces as the artists looked at each other. Only Julia Jansen had received none of that in the minutes before the ambulance had been able to sweep her away along with Rusty.

Krystal felt the sting of that distrust herself. She and her mother. They had created this place. They had made it possible for killers to thrive here.

They were as guilty as anyone.

Krystal felt her throat tighten as she looked at her mother. Joan sat in the chair beside her and the two women held hands tightly.

"That's it," Joan whispered. "They'll all leave soon and I doubt many will come back."

Krystal would have liked to argue the point but looking around she knew her mother was right. The Mountain Artists' Retreat at Cold Creek Canyon would bear this stain for a long time. Too long for the business to survive.

Not even a bear attack five years before had dried up the business. That was a natural threat, one they were all warned about before coming here. One that could be controlled by proper behavior, such as never ever feeding the bears.

This was entirely different. Unnatural. Something that could have been prevented, although just how Krystal couldn't imagine. Should they have allowed their clients to bring their own weapons? Hardly. The "no weapons" rule had its basis in protection of wildlife, prevention of accidents and even a genuine, if unstated, concern about a client who might get too drunk and too angry in some kind of argument.

No, that rule had been meant to protect, and the fact that it hadn't this time was not her mother's fault. No one could plan for a Mel or a Mary. But it wasn't going to matter where the fault lay, was it?

Krystal smothered a sigh and wished she could find a single word to cheer her mother up. None came.

Joan shook herself finally as the room nearly emptied. "We need to staple those curtains closed," she said briskly. "Keep the night out."

And the fears.

To her surprise, the remaining veterans immediately stepped in to help with the job. Two staple guns were dug out of the equipment storage room at the back and willing hands went to work. The dark curtains rippled forlornly even as they were stapled tight over broken glass.

The chandelier lighting still worked, creating its rustic glow as it always had. One of the vets started a fire in one of the fireplaces.

In a surprisingly short time, most everything looked natural again. Although it never would be.

Joan's kitchen, with the help of Donna and one of her helpers, began churning out frozen cinnamon rolls and biscuits for the vets and those who remained. The coffee machines began working overtime.

The remaining vets ate quickly, then sifted away into the outside world, a world they didn't want to share anymore, but a world they had just saved. Even Carly Narth, who had spent the dangerous hours beside Krystal, vanished as well. Krystal had wanted to thank her sincerely, but the opportunity was lost, for now.

Reject, happy with a biscuit, curled up on a chair and looked quite content. Krystal stroked him, thinking what a hero that husky was.

Maybe a dozen of their residents remained, talking quietly now, eating cinnamon rolls and drinking coffee.

Deciding the fate of the artists' retreat? Sharing the million reasons they would never return?

Joan walked over to them, pausing at each table for a conversation, although what her mother could say to change any minds after this Krystal couldn't imagine. But maybe she could. Some of these relationships stretched back for years.

And after a bit she saw a few faces smile. Okay, then. Maybe Joan could work a miracle.

For her part, the day was getting to her. Reject had curled up and gone to sleep and she so very much wanted to join him.

Except that after today she suspected her dreams would be nightmares, filled with all the horrors Mel and Mary had brought into her life. Into everyone's life.

They'd probably need to get a full-time psychologist just to deal with this aftermath.

Then she thought of Josh. He was a psychologist and apparently he now devoted his life to helping people who'd been through traumatic experiences. Although she suspected that what had happened at this lodge would never in any way reach the level of horror those vets had known.

Just look at Carly Narth with her badly burned body and head. God, the option of suicide had probably sounded good to her at times.

Despite not being able to fully relax, however, Krystal rested her head in her hand, elbow on the table, and began to drift into an uncomfortable sleep.

Then a voice drew her from the dawning of a nightmare.

"Krystal?" Josh, his voice quiet, almost gentle.

She pried her eyes open.

"I have to go. My people may need to help each other deal with what's just happened. I don't know how long it might take. Several days?"

Krystal managed a nod even as her heart sank. "They were brave," she said, although she could scarcely imagine how emotionally brave some had been, given their backgrounds and the troubles they faced now.

"Yes," Josh said. "They are. Do you want to stay here or do you want me to walk you back to your cabin?"

Oh, the peace of her cabin sounded so good just then, but she still saw Joan across the room.

"I need to stay," she told Josh. "There's an aftermath here, too. I don't want my mom to face it alone."

He nodded understanding. "I'll see you in a few days."

Then he was up, striding toward the door, his remaining two soldiers following him.

Back to their stockade. Back to the place where they had been trying to keep the world out.

God, it all stank.

Two people with a grudge had just psychologically wounded dozens. And to what end?

Chapter Thirteen

Josh saw Krystal often over the next week, but only from a distance. She had returned to her cabin and her habit of sitting outside with her morning coffee.

A plank walkway, chest-high, lined the interior walls of the stockade and he, too, returned to a morning ritual of pacing it with his coffee.

Between him and Krystal, Cash Creek roiled, still muddy from the storm, still carrying some debris from higher up. The stepping stones had vanished beneath racing water.

A boundary. Probably a good thing, given the thoughts that had been plaguing him.

His people were doing well, considering. They felt proud of what they had done, proud of facing their personal demons to do it. But pride notwithstanding, none showed the least inclination to leave the stockade walls again anytime soon.

The morning was chilly. Josh had found an old shearling jacket buried in his belongings and wore it instead of his usual camo jacket. Warm. Soft with age. The mug of coffee in his hands was growing cold, but he didn't care.

He was staring too much and too often at Krystal and she probably knew it. People always knew when someone was staring at them. He just hoped he wasn't making her uncomfortable. He kept looking away, training his gaze on something else, pretending that the forest out there was the most fascinating thing he'd ever seen.

And in a way it was. He had come here only because his family had owned this land and that piece of forest for generations. Then he got the letter from the Forest Service saying that the land appeared to be abandoned and would become part of the forest if no response was made within a year...

Well, it hadn't taken him long to come up with a great idea for this place. Isolated, the beauty of being surrounded by woods, the opportunity to perform tasks that suited each individual? Yeah. Perfect.

And so far it had been. Well, until the events of the last week. At least those seemed to have caused mere psychological ripples rather than the emotional tsunami he'd feared.

A few phone calls with Gage Dalton assured him the wheels of justice were grinding for Mel and Mary, but there'd be an inevitable need for testimony from his troops. Maybe they could take care of most of that out here? Gage said he'd make that possible insofar as he could.

Problems. Problems upon problems, but his gaze drifted back to Krystal again. So near yet so far. Maybe the biggest problem on his plate. Years ago he'd learned to let go of things to the extent that he could. Let go of people because they'd go away eventually.

Although there were faces and names he carried in his heart like burning brands. They'd never go away. But he'd made an uncomfortable peace with that.

So he ought to be able to turn his back on Krystal Metcalfe, right?

Except he didn't seem able to, even when he castigated himself with awareness of his own problems and limitations, and how little he had to offer a woman. A normal life? Hah. A family? He didn't know if he would dare.

Comfort and security? Well, security maybe. Comfort wasn't likely in this stockade. Nor would he consider leaving this structure or asking her to live here. People here depended on him and they had every right to. He'd given them the right.

He looked down at the central parade ground where his group had begun to move on to their daily chores.

His *friends*.

But the force that was drawing him toward Krystal was growing stronger by the hour. More irresistible.

Krystal ordinarily loved Cash Creek, but right now she loathed it. Sitting on her porch, booted feet up on the railing, coffee in hand, all she could see was a muddy gash that cut her off from Josh's stockade.

She was aware that he watched her sometimes. She watched him, too, when she thought she could avoid detection. Part of her felt extremely foolish, sure this was nothing more than the kind of crush she'd experienced in high school.

But her heart kept telling a different story. Even though she hardly knew the man, she knew she wanted him.

And not just physically. Something about Josh had reached past old barriers constructed to protect herself from heartache, a heartache experienced so long ago that she had all but forgotten it.

Apparently she hadn't. A boy she could barely remember, a summer romance shorter than the summer itself, had left a deep mark on her, a scar that had stayed with her although she rarely thought about it.

Until now. Now it rode her with warnings of heartbreak, barely remembered though it was.

Josh couldn't possibly want her anyway. She was nothing, a young woman who couldn't quite get her career on track, a woman whose life seemed tied up with a now dying business. A woman with a very limited future, it seemed.

What did she have to offer? He was a man of the world. He'd seen things she didn't even want to imagine, had lived a breadth of experience that made her own comfortable life dull by comparison. More importantly, he had devoted his life to an important cause. She certainly couldn't claim that.

Hell, what did she even have to talk to him about?

Separate worlds. Separate lives.

Divided as much by Cash Creek as anything right then.

She hated that creek. Then she shook her head at herself and headed inside for fresh coffee and another stab at a blank page on her computer screen.

What if she wrote about the nightmare they'd all just survived? At least it might clear the lingering cobwebs of the horror from her mind.

JOAN CALLED A few hours later. The mountain afternoon was turning chilly as it often did, and Krystal had wrapped herself in a blue fleece sweater, one long enough it reached her knees.

"Well," Joan said, "you'll be amazed to know that I'm

getting some reservations for this winter. From some of last year's visitors. And some, believe it or not, from people who were here with us during that horror."

That horror. Neither of them seemed able to describe it any other way.

Krystal's heart leaped happily. "That's great, Mom. I guess some folks aren't thinking that any of that was the fault of the retreat."

Joan sighed. "I could easily see how some of them might. You were right when you said I should have stopped inviting Mason."

"As if anyone could have predicted this. Really? I just wanted him gone because he was so irritating. Too irritating apparently."

"Mary Collins must have thought he was more than irritating. Anyway, I still can't believe that a resentment could flower into that horror."

That horror. "I think flower might be the wrong word."

Joan laughed. "You are *so* right. So when are you coming up here again? I know there's going to be a lot of banging for a few days to repair those windows, but *I'm* here to entertain you."

"Tomorrow morning," Krystal promised. "After my morning coffee."

After the call, she once again regarded the roiled creek with displeasure and peered over her coffee cup at Josh Healey.

Oh, man, did she have it bad. And he probably hardly knew she existed anymore, even though she caught him sometimes looking her way from his stockade. Nope. He was probably thinking about other things. As proved by his disappearance from the walkway, gone on to other occupations.

A week. Slightly more. Not even a wave across the canyon.

Sighing, she threw hope to the winds and returned to that blank screen in front of her. Where to start writing about those terrible events?

Before she could think of a single word to type, however, someone knocked on her door. Startled, she jumped up. In an instant she realized her sense of safety had been badly damaged by the events with Mel and Mary.

It was just her door. Just her *door*. She'd never hesitated to open it before, but now she stared at it as if a poisonous snake waited beyond.

God, she couldn't allow this to continue, to allow her entire life to be permanently altered by those two beasts.

It was just a knock on the door, for heaven's sake. It was probably someone from the lodge bearing some food gift from Joan's kitchen, where Donna and her help seemed to be determined to produce menus fit for a king, few guests as they had at the moment.

The knock came again. "Krystal?"

It was Josh. Her heart nearly stopped and she froze in place. Part of her wondered how he'd crossed the creek, part of her skittered around inside her head trying to figure out what he could possibly want here. Most of her was afraid of what he might *not* want here.

"Krystal? Are you okay?"

At last she managed to shake herself free of conflicting thoughts. Just a neighborly visit. Nothing more. Maybe he needed a cup of sugar?

At that, the last of her tension seeped away and she grinned at herself. Much better.

She took the three steps and opened the plank door. Josh stood there, wearing jeans and a shearling jacket and muddy rubber boots up to his knees.

"Hi," he said with a half smile. "You busy?"

"Um...no. But how'd you cross that creek?"

His smile widened. "I found a place upstream that wasn't too bad. I'll keep my muddy boots out here, though."

"Coffee? I can bring it out."

"Sounds great." He moved to sit in one of her Adirondack chairs.

But before she stepped inside, she turned to look straight at him. "Why," she asked nervously, afraid of his answer, "did you hunt up a way to cross the creek?"

He tilted his head slightly, then shrugged, his expression growing inscrutable. "Seemed there was this lady on the other side of the creek and I couldn't stop thinking about getting over here to see her."

Her heart stopped for the second time in just a few minutes and she slowly sat on the edge of the other chair, coffee forgotten. The creek rushed below, swallowing sound, nearly silencing a breeze that began to blow in the treetops.

"Josh?" Her voice trembled, then her hands shook as well.

"I know this is nuts," he said, his face still unreadable. "You have every right to tell me to swim back across that creek and never show my face again. I mean, look at all those people across the way that I'm working with. Who'd want to take that on?"

Krystal caught her breath and her hands knotted together. She hardly dared to allow her imagination to fill in the blanks in what he was saying. Or what he hadn't said.

But small tendrils of hope began to grow in her heart. Josh… She couldn't even explain to herself what was happening inside her.

He waved a hand. "Sorry. I'm naturally ham-handed when it comes to talking about my feelings. Wouldn't have thought this would be harder than a group therapy session."

"Harder?" Her nails were beginning to dig into her palms as every bit of fear and nervousness tiptoed its way to hope.

"I get that you don't know me," he continued almost roughly. "How could you? We're basically strangers to each other."

She couldn't dispute that and hope began to slip away. Just a little.

"But we have time to talk ourselves blue in the face if we want to. The thing is, Krystal, do you want to?"

Something sucked nearly all the air from the universe. Krystal's heart hammered, her voice grew thready. "Want to?"

"Get to know me. Me to get to know you. I know it won't be easy because I won't give up my soldiers for any reason, but we can cross that line if we get to it. In the meantime, we need to talk to each other. We can give those damn stepping stones a real workout."

Then he astonished her, rising from his chair to come kneel right in front of her and take her cold hands in his large, warm ones.

"Like I said," he repeated huskily, "I'm ham-handed when it comes to stuff like this. But, Krystal, you're haunting my dreams and damn near every waking moment. You have me thinking about things I haven't considered in years. Things like a family. A future. And I want them with you."

That's when he let go of her. "I guess this would be a good time to leave."

She reached for his hands, grabbing them tightly as she pulled them back. "Why?"

"Why should I go?" He shook his head. "Dang, Krystal, I'm damn near a perfect stranger, I just marched into your house and threw a whole bunch of emotions at your feet and I have no business to expect anything but a heave-ho."

But every barrier, every fear, every uncertainty inside Krystal washed away like the crashing water on Cash Creek. She rose to her feet, wrapped her arms around his shoulders and pulled him close to her as an indescribable joy rushed through her.

"Damn it, Josh, don't you dare think of leaving, I've been craving you, too, and you'll break my heart if you…"

He didn't let her finish. He stood, sweeping her off her feet, a huge smile on his face. "Screw the mud," he said as he headed for the door and the interior of her house, "I'll clean it up later. The only thing I care about right now is loving you with every ounce of my being."

"Oh, yeah," she said, leaning her head into his shoulder and grabbing the front of his shirt tightly. "Please. And promise never to stop."

"Never," he said as he kissed her deeply.

Only the second of many, many more to come.

"I love you," she whispered, surprised at the words that

escaped her heart, words she had been for so long afraid to say.

"I love you, too," he said gruffly. "Impossible, yeah? No. It's here, it's now."

Then he added, "It's here forever."

* * * * *